Brief ENCOUNTERS

YI MUN-YOL

Yi Mun-yol was born in 1948. During the Korean War (1950-3), his father supported the North Korean side for ideological reasons and went to live in the North, leaving his family in the South. In his youth, Yi Mun-yol had to bear the stigma of being a 'traitor's son'. With more than thirty books published and sales totalling many millions of copies, Yi Mun-yol is Korea's leading novelist. *The Poet*, his most significant novel, has been translated into all the major western languages.

ALSO BY YI MUN-YOL

Meeting with My Brother

Our Twisted Hero

Son of Man

YI MUN-YOL

THE POET

Translated from the Korean by
Chong-wha Chung and Brother Anthony of Taizé

Brief ENCOUNTERS
VINTAGE CLASSICS

1 3 5 7 9 10 8 6 4 2

Vintage Classics is part of the Penguin Random House group of companies

Vintage, Penguin Random House UK, One Embassy Gardens,
8 Viaduct Gardens, London SW11 7BW

penguin.co.uk/vintage-classics
global.penguinrandomhouse.com

This edition published in Vintage Classics in 2026
First published in Great Britain by The Harvill Press in 1995
First published in Korea with the title *Shiin* in 1992

This edition is published with the kind assistance of the Korean Culture and Arts Foundation

Map drawn by Leslie Robinson

Set in 10.9/13pt Bembo Book MT Pro
Typeset by Six Red Marbles UK, Thetford, Norfolk

Printed and bound in Great Britain by Clays Ltd, Elcograf S.p.A.

The authorised representative in the EEA is Penguin Random House Ireland,
Morrison Chambers, 32 Nassau Street, Dublin D02 YH68

A CIP catalogue record for this book is available from the British Library

ISBN 9781529986112

Penguin Random House is committed to a sustainable future
for our business, our readers and our planet. This book is made
from Forest Stewardship Council® certified paper.

Contents

Author's Preface

It was in the summer of 1984 that I first became interested in the life of that unique poet Kim the Bamboo Hat, as a literary topic. I had previously read and heard a fair amount about him, but what provoked my sudden literary interest that year may have been the controversy surrounding the publication of my *Tong-ung Si-dae* (*Heroic Age*). There is a risk of over-simplification, but essentially *Heroic Age* represents a disavowal of my own father, and people generally believe that the original reason forcing Kim out into a life of wandering was something similar.

Once my interest was aroused and I began to look more closely, I realized that there were many more fascinating and impressive aspects to Kim's life than I had thought. In particular, the political and social messages buried in the legends sometimes made me shudder.

The first thing that attracted my attention was the region in which he had begun his wanderings. From the time he left home when he was in his mid-twenties until he reached his mid-thirties, he spent the whole time wandering through the provinces of Hamkyong and Pyongan, frequenting in particular many of the places connected with Hong Kyong-rae's uprising. Even with no other explanation, that suggested strongly what must have been the origin of his youthful torment and despair. I was moved to tears to read how, during a visit to Dabok Village, he had wept aloud on confessing that he was Kim Ik-sun's grandson.

Yet if I decided to compose a new novel based on his life, it was only after I read documents telling how he had spent some time in his youth as a guest in a powerful household in an attempt to gain social promotion. Actually, that particular report is not recognized as authentic by some scholars, since it seems hard to square it with the life found in the legends, where he seems to be intent on freeing himself from all worldly attachments and bonds; yet I had no hesitation in choosing those documents for my basic material. Indeed, whenever I read the legends about him, the one thing I could clearly understand was that story, normally characterized as dubious.

At first I intended to write one novella and four or five short stories dealing with his life. The reason for rejecting the full-length-novel form was the thought that many such works had already appeared and there was the possibility of wearying the readers by repetition.

Once writing began, however, my ambitions grew and I found myself giving preference to a complex of emotions rather than one single effect, so that in the end I was led to write a full-length novel. I only hope that this change of scale has not weighed too heavily on the work. In addition, that change occurred in the course of composition, and I was caught between the deadlines imposed by the magazine in which instalments were being published, and the increased length of the work, so that I was forced to do the impossible, which merely adds to my concern. I can only ask for the reader's understanding.

Yi Mun-yol

Korea at the time of Kim Sakkat

I

Perhaps we ought to begin this investigation into the deviations of his life by evoking the problem of memory. In his later years, summing up the whole course of his existence in a long lyric, he wrote the following lines:

As my hair grew longer,
  my fortunes travelled a rough road:
The family line in ruins,
  the blue sea a mulberry grove.

Later readers have not usually considered those lines to be the transposition into poetry of any actual experience. At most they have assumed that they were inspired by some childhood event he learned about in his adult years, a pseudo-memory as it were, an analogy fabricated to harmonize with the presumed course of his life's history.

Such theories may satisfy those who prefer an entertaining folktale to the actual details of a man's life. For them, it is unthinkable that he might have retained any actual memories of his family or origins before that fateful moment, so often chronicled, when he won first prize in a rural poetry contest at the age of nineteen. That way the legend could be given a dramatic and really effective starting-point.

Unfortunately, the realities of life rarely if ever correspond to the demands of such fabulations. Generally received opinion notwithstanding, his memory actually stretched much further back into the past than is normally the case.

In particular, even when his life was almost done, at the end when he was weary and alone, he could recall the events of a certain evening late in the year in which he turned four as vividly as if they were just then happening before his eyes: that fateful night when his life was fundamentally transformed, as if the blue sea had indeed suddenly been turned into a mulberry grove.

He was only a child, of course, but during the last few days he had become vaguely aware of an extraordinary atmosphere brooding over the house.

The servants who had until then filled their home with a constant presence seemed visibly to have diminished in number, while those who remained no longer worked but stood in corners endlessly whispering together.

It was only an uncertain memory, but it seemed that sometimes words like "rebellion" and "his Lordship" could be heard emerging from the whispers. Among those days' strange memories was one of his father, who normally remained in his quarters, lying down more often than sitting up, busily going about on visits solemnly dressed in formal attire.

That day too his father had listened to a message that a steward, rushing in from somewhere, had whispered, and then gone out without bothering to adjust his dress, walking with quick steps down the already darkening street. More than anything else, the sight of his father's retreating figure made the atmosphere he sensed about the house seem darker and heavier, as if there was about to be a shattering explosion.

That was why, although night had fallen, he did not go across to the room he shared with his elder brother in the outer quarters, but lingered on in the women's rooms. No supper was brought in, but he stayed there beside his mother who was shivering slightly as she hugged and rocked his tiny newborn brother.

He might have been rather more sensitive than other children but still he was only four. Inevitably, as the evening wore on, despite the ominous trembling he could feel through the hem of his mother's skirts that he was grasping, he began to doze.

It was almost as if he had invited sleep to come in an attempt to escape from the suffocating stillness that reigned in the house and the incomprehensible suspense, but that must have been an idea he introduced when he was older.

His father returned just as he was about to give up the fight against sleep and stretch out with his head pillowed on his mother's knees. A wave of cold air from outside clinging to his robes came billowing round the room, as his father addressed him curtly:

"Go over to your room now, Pyong-yon."

In the light of the guttering candle his father's face was so pale it looked almost livid. It was such a fearful pallor that there could be no question of answering back, let alone of wheedling to stay.

He crossed the hall, dimly lit by a hanging lantern, with the wind making a mournful sound as it brushed across the wide inner courtyard; he had already taken off his slippers and the feel of the icy wood against the soles of his bare feet would long remain one of that night's most vivid memories. His brother Pyong-ha was sitting there alone in their room, which for no apparent reason struck cold as he opened the door. Perhaps his big six-year-old brother had different feelings to his?

"Is father back?"

His brother asked the question, looking at him as he came in, like someone roused out of deep thoughts. Feeling for some reason that it would be wrong to reply in words, he simply nodded silently. Perhaps what he was feeling had communicated itself to his brother and for some time he did not speak. But his brother seemed to have something he needed to say, words that he could not endure to keep bottled up inside him.

"It seems half the servants have already run away."

His brother spoke in a whisper, like someone revealing a great secret. It was something he had already realized to some degree, but as soon as his brother spoke he found himself longing to know the reason for it.

"Why have they run away? What reason is there for the servants to leave?"

He too lowered his voice; his brother seemed perplexed for a moment. In retrospect, his perplexity may have come from a feeling that he knew why but should not say it, or that if he spoke his brother might not understand; there was an element of sibling superiority involved.

A moment later, his brother seemed to have made up his mind and was going to explain; but there was not a single word that he remembered having heard. For just as his brother was about to speak, their mother's sobbing voice rang abruptly across the courtyard.

The two of them suddenly seemed to have matured by several years; as they listened in anxious silence, their mother's sobs gradually changed into a muffled keening. But almost at once the bedroom door opened, then slammed shut in response to their father's low command, and the sound of their mother's weeping began slowly to diminish.

Once again an ominous silence pressed heavily on the household. Becoming for no apparent reason more serious than ever, the brothers strained their ears towards the inner quarters, but the only sound that reached them was from time to time the squeak of a wardrobe hinge or the creak of a drawer being opened then shut.

A little later they heard their mother's footsteps crossing the hall. When she opened the door, her face showed no trace of tears.

"Pyong-ha, change into these."

She thrust a set of thick clothing at his elder brother and then helped him change too. He disliked the chill feeling as he put them on, but the quilted clothes quickly grew warm.

Even the slippers on his feet were double and padded; then, just as his mother was winding a silk scarf about his head, the door opened again and their father came in, his breath steaming white, together with Su-man.

Su-man was a young servant who had been a palanquin-bearer in the days when their grandfather had a position in the capital, but at present his function was to look after the men's quarters. While their father only looked haggard, Su-man's dark red face was shining with an endless flow of tears, there was something animal-like about it.

"When you get to Koksan, tell Kim Song-su that he's no longer a serf for our family; he's a respectable free citizen now. And tell him that the land there doesn't belong to me any more, but to him.

Tell him, too, not to make too much of a burden of raising these two boys. Just so long as they survive, and I'm not guilty of putting an end to the family line: I can't hope for more."

Their father repeated once more to Su-man instructions that he seemed already to have given him several times before, then turned and looked at the two brothers.

"You don't belong to an influential family any longer; you're no longer my sons. From now on you're going to live as the sons of Kim Song-su, a freed serf. You're on your way home to Koksan in Hwanghae Province. You're returning after a visit to your mother's family and you're the nephews of Chon Su-man here. Do you understand?"

There was something moist about their father's voice, unlike its usual tone. He stopped speaking and they all waited. A moment later he cleared his throat and regained his habitual serenity.

"Do you understand? Your father is Kim Song-su of Koksan district in Hwanghae Province. You've been visiting your mother's family in Yongin and now you're on your way back home with your uncle, you're going to celebrate the New Year there. In future you must never regard your father's or grandfather's name as your own."

On reflection, their father cannot have been even thirty at the time. How to explain the composure he showed while taking his leave of those two young sons that he would probably never see again, at an age when it is no easy thing to control one's emotions? Was it due to his strong self-control? Or the dignity expected of even a run-of-the-mill gentleman? Or did he secretly believe, despite what he said, that they would sooner or later be reunited?

In any case, the solemnity and dignity conveyed by those words were sufficient to overwhelm the young brothers. They had the feeling of some kind of ineluctable destiny, not only from the strange atmosphere or this abrupt departure that they had known nothing about, but above all from the way their father spoke.

The father shot a glance at their mother. Despite all her efforts to restrain them, tears were dripping down on to the ribbons on the front of her dress; then once again he addressed Su-man. The main substance of his father's words also remained in his memory until the very end of his life.

"You don't have to come back. Once you've given these children over to Song-su, go your own way. I burned your serf's papers with those of Song-su, so no one's going to come after you. With the gold I gave you, you'll be able to find a scrap of land, no matter where you go, big enough to feed and house yourself, so you don't have to feel any loyalty to this fallen family."

This was his father as he used to be, not on the days when he couldn't take any more and stayed lying down, but when he would sit high up in his room, well-groomed and correct. The only memory of his father he preserved from before then was of times when, if he made even a little noise playing in the garden of the men's quarters, a window would slide open and a hand silently wave him away. If they had separated then and there, he would probably have remembered his father in later times for his coldness.

But his father was incapable of keeping his heartbroken feelings hidden to the end. It was just as he was being carried on Su-man's back through the middle gate:

"Take care of yourselves. Poor little things. If heaven is not too cruel, we'll meet again some day . . ."

Those few words, blurted out at the last moment after he had followed them as far as he intended, sounded more pathetic than any tears. Their mother's sobbing burst out again behind their father as he spoke; it followed them for a while along the road.

2

He could never identify precisely the emotion that dominated him that evening. No matter how hard he racked his memories in later years, he could find no sign that he had begged or shed tears in an effort not to go, as he was parted from his father and mother.

He was only four; suddenly he was separated from his parents, without knowing why, and sent off to an unknown destination; with a feeling moreover that he might never see them again . . .

Strange though it may seem, perhaps a fear of death had

seized his infant soul at that moment. Had he not instinctively realized, although he had never heard anyone talk about dying, that what he was escaping from was precisely that thing called death?

He may have been terrified of something, but it seemed to be by no means as precise a fear as that which his brother Pyong-ha was feeling. His brother had been following Su-man without a word as he almost ran along in his effort to get away from that neighbourhood, carrying the younger boy on his back. As they followed the dark streets, he suddenly asked:

"Why do we have to run away like this?"

"Because . . . young master . . ."

Su-man stopped abruptly and restrained his harsh breathing, while hesitating to give a clear answer. Their father's words had obviously not yet become real for his brother, he spoke as if nothing had changed, demanding a reply:

"Tell us. What's happening?"

"I'm not sure that you're old enough to understand, young masters."

"I order you to tell us."

"Do you know that a great revolt has broken out in the north? The people in Pyongan Province have plotted sedition, and have risen up . . ."

"I gathered as much from what the servants were whispering."

"But his Lordship who was stationed in Sonchon . . ."

"What has our grandfather done?"

"He was captured by the rebels – and they say he surrendered to them. But you know that anyone surrendering to rebels becomes a rebel, too."

"But then why are we . . .?"

Judging by his questions his older brother was rather slowwitted for his age. Or else the younger brother was far too bright. The only thing he had really studied were the first thousand Chinese characters – which he had learned while playing on his grandmother's lap. Yet by now he already knew: if someone becomes a rebel, the punishment entails the destruction of that person's family for three generations, and they were included in that.

In the end, his brother stopped asking questions, after he had heard Su-man's stammering replies:

"I am very sorry, young master . . . by law, a rebel's whole family must be exterminated. Young masters . . . now we're escaping from that. Your father's orders . . . you haven't forgotten, have you? From now on, you're not your father's sons any longer, not your grandfather's grandsons. Now you're going to have to take the man we're on our way to . . . as your father, and live as his sons. It's the only way . . . to save your lives."

When they came close to Sowi Gate, the faint sound of the drum signal heralding the lifting of the curfew reached their ears, but the endless winter's night was still as dark as ever. Here and there around the gate fires had been lit and even from a distance they could make out soldiers on watch, coming and going. Su-man's whole body flinched, and he whispered in a tense voice:

"They say there are people in collusion with the rebels in the city, too. Young masters, let's get some rest in that tavern over there, and go on when day breaks. The guards will most likely think it strange if they see someone trying to slip out with young children at the crack of dawn . . ."

As he led the brothers towards the tavern, he added with an apologetic air:

"From now on, it's as your father ordered, I'm your maternal uncle. That means I'll have to use the language of an uncle to you, and you must speak in honorific forms to me. First we'll practise on the innkeeper, then we'll do the same with the soldiers as we leave the city."

Su-man's words caused the younger boy, who was still perched on his back, no vexation, not even the slightest stir of refusal, and his brother seemed to be feeling the same. So when Su-man suddenly began to speak to them in disrespectful tones as he entered the inn, his older brother followed along behind saying "Yes, uncle; yes, sir," as if he had been doing it for a long time. Perhaps his brother had glimpsed a few moments before, as he had, the substance of the fear pursuing them in the firelight gleaming reflected on the points of the soldiers' spears.

3

Even when he was very old, it took only a slight effort of will for him to be able to picture vividly every stage of their ten-day journey to Koksan. Sleet had begun to fall as they were leaving Sowi Gate, and it became heavier at about the time they took the road leading towards Koyang County, finally turning into a real blizzard. After a night spent at the inn in Pyokjae, the snow had still not stopped.

The next day was the same, and the next . . . so that as they were approaching Hwanghae Province, the whole world seemed to be covered with snow.

How is it that snow has the power to make everything so generously, so marvellously beautiful? Although the accumulation of several years' poor harvests had in the end become a major factor in producing large-scale rebellion, the bright snow-covered plains of Yonbaek had nothing arid or dreary about them.

If he had not been so weary on account of the unreasonable pace Su-man kept up, surely that pure white expanse of fields, so utterly beautiful, would long have remained engraved in his mind.

When they arrived at places where houses clustered together to form villages, his memories were different again. The houses were obviously inhabited, yet the villages seemed oddly cold and silent. As they passed through hamlets in which not even a dog could be heard barking, the people they saw seemed afraid, looking furtively at them and not speaking; even if they entered an inn, it was rare indeed to find a smiling landlady or even a place capable of serving a proper meal.

He learned only later that large battalions of government forces had repeatedly gone through those villages, stripping them bare after they had already been impoverished by an accumulation of poor harvests and, worse still, by the exactions of local magnates.

These troops from the capital had been sent all over Pyongan Province as reinforcements designed to cut off the rebel army's last lifeline. They had not only emptied the villages of their cows, chickens, and dogs, they had not hesitated to take even the few measures of grain that farmers had hidden to tide themselves over until spring came.

Nothing, though, could equal the vividness of his memories of the hardship the three of them suffered along the way. Sturdy youth though he was, it was no easy task for Su-man to bring those two children, one nearly five and one a few days short of seven, on a winter journey of about eighty miles.

Pyong-ha, the elder brother, bore up well for the first day, but on the second he began to complain that his legs were hurting, and Su-man was obliged to carry them in turns on his back the rest of the way. A long, tedious journey! When they were being carried, their feet were cold, and when they were walking, their legs hurt. The joy when, on rounding some mountain spur, they spied what looked like a tavern in the distance, was greater than anything he ever felt in his later years of wandering.

No less than the hardship of walking was the anxiety they experienced each time they were obliged to take a ferry or pass a checkpoint. To avoid the furtive glances of a ferryman or the fierce stares of police and soldiers, they sometimes chose to make a detour of three or four miles.

Even after wandering had become a major feature of his life, he experienced a fit of panic every time he was confronted with a river-crossing or a checkpoint; that must surely have been because memories of his childhood lay buried somewhere deep inside his soul.

Su-man proved himself a wise and faithful servant, worthy of the charge entrusted to him by their father. He carried the two brothers turn by turn on his back without any pause for well over eighty miles, and brought them safely to Kim Song-su in his home at Hwachon in Koksan just as the sun was setting, a few days before the end of the year.

Su-man handed the two over to Kim Song-su as if he was freeing himself of a precious and weighty burden. Then he lay down and slept without a break for one whole night and one whole day in a room with a dirt-floor, before he left.

He only ever met Su-man once after that, more than twenty years later. That was when he was wandering through Hamkyong

Province, and Su-man was already an elderly man living in a mountain village far up in Tongchon; there was no way he could refuse his invitation. He spent five days with him; when he finally left, Su-man accompanied him for more than a mile along the road, not once letting go of the hem of his coat.

4

Kim Song-su proved to be fully Su-man's equal in faithfulness to his former master. It was nearly the end of the Choson Era, a time when the social order was breaking down completely, and a flood of alarming stories was circulating, including some about a former serf who had secretly murdered his master when he came on a visit from a distant place.

Certainly Kim Song-su was in a position to act very differently toward the two brothers. After all, the first thing he heard from Su-man on his arrival was that his former master had burned his document of bondage, then he received legal ownership of the plot of land he was cultivating. There was absolutely no legal provision that could have forced him to accept the costly and troublesome task of bringing up the two boys; even if there had been, his former master was by then nothing more than a traitor's son, and as such lay outside the protection of all laws and institutions.

Besides, at that time the rebellion had still not been completely put down, so that if he had taken the two brothers and handed them over to the local authorities, he could have looked forward to a considerable reward.

In fact though, Kim Song-su faithfully did as he had been requested without the least hesitation, although it was highly doubtful whether his former master was still alive by that time. Indeed, later, when they were back at their parents' house, they often used to refer to him as their "Koksan father" with considerable affection, no doubt because his faithful service had deeply touched their infant hearts.

Still, that could not protect them from suffering under the many kinds of deprivation that they had to endure during the more than two years they spent in Koksan. To be sure, Kim Song-su followed very precisely their father's orders; but on the other hand, on account of the limited understanding only to be expected in a serf who had always lived a humble life, he sometimes inflicted hurts on them, and at times might have given them cause to harbour deep resentment.

One thing they found infinitely displeasing in the early days was the way Kim Song-su acted as if he really was their father. He insisted on being called "Father", and even had the malicious pleasure of deceiving the old woman who had recently come to live with him by presenting the brothers as his own children by a first, deceased wife. Inevitably, too, doubts arose when they found themselves forced to take off their silk clothes and cotton shoes and put on instead unlined cotton jackets and straw shoes without socks, before being sent out into the wintry yard to play.

They felt deeply humiliated when they were given commoners' nicknames in place of their aristocratic names. As they sat picking at the coarse food they were not yet used to, Kim Song-su's loud scolding used to make them grind their teeth.

He had been prepared by Su-man during the journey, so he put up with Kim Song-su's use of discourteous forms of language in addressing them; but when he poured out torrents of vulgar abuse, irrespective of whether other people were around or not, scolding them for some small faults, as if that country bumpkin were their real father, it was so hurtful that his eyes would fill with tears.

There were other painful things in living as Kim Song-su's sons, too. Three days after coming there, they were given the job of lighting the fire to cook the cattle-feed; ten days after that the whole task of chopping the fodder and cooking the cattle-feed was passed on to them from the old woman.

When spring came, Kim Song-su was off to the fields with the brothers; and he set to work training them as farm hands at a rather earlier age than other farming fathers trained their sons.

Perhaps, although they were still young, if the two brothers had realized a little more clearly that the land Kim Song-su was cultivating really formed part of their own lost inheritance, and that like

Su-man he himself was nothing more than a serf inherited from their grandparents' generation, it might have been hard for them to accept such treatment from him without accumulating deep feelings of resentment.

More than that, if their childish hearts had not been dominated, instinctively, by fear of a death which seemed more terrible still by reason of its abstract quality, or if they had made any other choice, those two upper-class children would almost certainly never have endured their sudden fall into utter misery, after beginning life in the midst of so much loving care and devoted service.

Kim Song-su, though, was convinced that such treatment was the only way to protect the boys from his neighbours' suspicion, and fortunately they vaguely recognized his sincerity in acting as he did, so that nothing irreparable happened. There was also another occasion when Kim Song-su was able at least temporarily to play a paternal role in the two brothers' memories.

It occurred in the early spring, just over two years after their arrival in Koksan. Kim Song-su, who could not tell a T from a hammer, one day suddenly took the two boys along to enrol them in the village school. His was a tight enough situation, what with residence taxes, defence tax, and goodness knows what else to be paid; sending them to school on top of that, where the basic charge alone was two sacks of rice, was near-madness in the eyes of his neighbours.

Kim Song-su never explained clearly, even later, why that new idea suddenly came to him. All things duly considered, perhaps he had heard a report that the authorities had in the end decided to spare the family; his action may also have been prompted by a feeling that he had not shown enough gratitude for his former master's generosity.

If really he acted out of a realization that a true repayment for generosity would mean not merely saving the brothers' lives but training their minds, to prepare them for the recovery of their family's former honour, that can only be considered a sign of a very considerable maturity on the part of Kim Song-su, who had after all spent his whole life as someone else's serf.

5

In the comic poems he wrote later, he is all the time mocking and making fun of the teachers at village schools. If you think for a moment, it is not hard to guess where his malice and contempt towards them came from.

In the course of the later Choson period the village schools had gradually declined, while still preserving their status as the chief institutions for the transmission of learning; they were generally staffed by local scholars who for one reason or another had been eliminated from the mainstream of promotion in society, who were incapable of rising higher on the social scale than the general certificate of learning. The fact of the matter was that the schools had deteriorated from their original function, and were now merely the easiest, indeed almost the only means by which second-rate intellectuals could make a living.

As the civil-service examination system was gradually corrupted by powerful clan interests, that degradation became far more severe. The lesser gentry, those having no connections with powerful families and without the financial means to bribe the examiners, gave up all hope of a career in the administration; instead, they went out into every rural nook and cranny to set up schools where they survived by selling their half-baked learning for next to nothing.

Then when the schoolmaster went to collect his year's tuition fee, which was fixed at the not-so-excessive amount of "one sack of rice and one copper penny", from the fathers of his pupils (most of them were low-ranking public officials), as often as not they would roll up their sleeves, frown and swear, and he would end up fleeing from the village "as if he had a tiger after him". Such was the age he was living in, it was inevitable that he should be more or less influenced by that same kind of social attitude.

The way in which he was in direct competition with those schoolmasters during his adult life, generally spent wandering from place to place, may very largely explain his ill-will towards them. Those teachers were mostly wandering scholars like himself; usually they would make a contract and stay between six months and one year in a place; even if the local people were highly satisfied, it was almost unknown for one to last more than three years.

As a result, when he entered a village it was only natural that the local schoolmaster should see him as a potential rival; that is why there were so many instances when he encountered quite uncalled-for hostility or surliness. As a matter of fact, from time to time he stayed on in a place and performed the functions of a teacher himself.

On the other hand, no matter what village in whatever remote valley he arrived at, the educated person he could most easily search out was precisely the local schoolmaster. Wherever he went he had necessarily at first to depend on the understanding and goodwill of the literate people he might find, which meant he was obliged to visit them first, but such a circumstance only helped foster his ill-will. For it is sure that if you have frequent encounters with members of one particular class, especially if you are looking to them for some kind of help at a time when everyone is experiencing hardship, you are obviously very often going to receive painful mistreatment at their hands.

His poetry, too, for which he very soon acquired a high reputation, was equally a cause of his deep contempt for those teachers. The mere sight of them was bound to be both revolting and comic, as they went swaggering around before the ignorant peasants, poetry and learning dangling from their noses, while really all they had was a little learning, a meagre talent, and low minds.

But one of the main factors, one that cannot be excluded from the reasons underlying his scorn and contempt for village teachers, is the negative impression he received from the master at the school there in Koksan. On the day Kim Song-su took them along to the school, the first question the master asked, all goatee beard and mousy eyes, was how soon he could pay half the fees.

When Kim Song-su asked him to wait three months, the next question was about his standard of living, and the next about where his family was from. He did not even once glance at the two brothers, or enquire about what they had learned or if they could write. Perhaps because he was still very young, much had grown hazy in the course of the last two years, but he could not detect the slightest trace of a scholar-gentleman's mien in that teacher, as he recalled it from still lingering memories of the scholars who had come visiting the guest rooms in their former home.

It was no different on the second day, when they had been squeezed in among the other pupils. Taking them for the children of poor peasants, the teacher placed them in the most remote corner, did not even try to find out anything about them, and forced them both to work through the primer from the beginning. Now the younger brother already knew most of its contents at least vaguely, while the elder of the two had almost completely mastered the book back in their old home.

Yet that teacher, constantly losing his temper whether they knew the answers or not, forced them to stick with the same primer until they left Koksan six months later. At a guess, he probably wanted to wait until there were other pupils ready to start the elementary level with them.

That master's fits of elation and of temper, the favours and rejections he meted out had nothing to do with how much or little talent or application a pupil displayed. If a piece of quite indifferent writing was produced by the son of some well-heeled local gentleman holding a modest post in the administration, it was glorified as "a fine composition", the child became "an infant prodigy"! Whereas if boys of poor commoners like the two brothers so much as stumbled over one insignificant phrase in reciting their lesson, he would explode into a fury as violent as if he had just suffered some kind of deep betrayal, lashing out with his cane.

To say nothing of the greed that kept that master's fleshy lips for ever on the move, the servile obsequiousness he showed before minor local dignitaries who had bought themselves sinecures with impressive-sounding titles, as well as the little learning manifested by his outbursts of anger if he could not find an answer to a boy's question . . .

All these various failings of their master surely underlie the jaundiced view he later showed towards schoolmasters in general; they were the cause of a revolt at the time, too. The two brothers soon lost all pleasure in the studies they had so eagerly begun, using every pretext to stay away from classes. It almost seems as though the younger was already beginning to cultivate the first tender shoots of what was later to become his complete alienation from the ways of society.

Fortunately, this early deviation on the part of the brothers was not destined to last for long. It was an early summer day that year. Once again, the two boys had got one of their schoolfellows living nearby to transmit a plausible-sounding excuse for their absence, then they had set off for the banks of the South River just below Hwachon.

Early as it was, they played in the water like two typical country lads, one now seven and the other nine, going dashing after swarms of minnows where the stream narrowed, then rummaging through the waterside thickets in quest of birds' eggs. As midday drew near, though, they began to be bored with one thing after another. The sun was becoming increasingly fierce, too, so that they could no longer play beside the river where they had no shade.

They were forced to shift their playground up under the willows on the embankment. They were longing to go back home but it was still too early for that. Their schoolmaster always ended lessons late, realizing that he only had to keep the boys sitting in the schoolroom for a long time for their families to be convinced that he was a first-class teacher.

Pyong-ha seemed to have worn himself out playing; no sooner had they moved into the shade than he lay down, cradled his head on one arm, and went to sleep.

Leaning against a tree with no special thought in mind, the younger brother gazed up at the billowing summer clouds as they unfolded in the blue sky overhead. The clouds he really liked best of all were those that went streaming restlessly across the sky in the breezes of autumn, but now he came to observe them quietly, these early summer clouds had their own kind of beauty, fashioning themselves now into flower buds, now into mountain ranges.

He was still only seven, though, and like any other child he could never stand still for a moment; the same was true of his thoughts. He suddenly wearied of looking at the clouds. In a flash, his mind turned to his own situation and suddenly he was longing for his parents, not knowing if they were alive or dead. Memories of his early childhood arose confusedly and for no particular reason he recalled their old home. It seemed palatial now, with servants hurrying busily to and fro.

He was just sinking into a strange state of melancholy musing when suddenly Kim Song-su seemed to come rising out of the ground and was standing there in the shadow of the trees. He had obviously heard what they were up to and had come running; without any warning he woke Pyong-ha with a box on the ear then, holding them by the scruff of the neck, one in each hand, he began to roar.

"Scoundrels! Good for nothing scoundrels! Is this your idea of school? Here, by the river? You dare go skiving off in the middle of classes when your father is breaking his back working to send you there?"

All the while he was being shaken by the neck, yet he could not help noticing out of one corner of his eye how a group of women, who had been washing clothes in the river not far away, were all laughing and screwing up their eyes tightly as if to say, "It serves you right!" Presumably one of them, finishing her washing early, had gone and dropped a hint to the old woman who lived with Kim Song-su.

Given what had happened, Kim Song-su duly did everything that a father is expected to do in such circumstances. As he dragged them home like two little puppies he poured out a stream of reproaches in a loud voice, then began to lament his fate, beating his breast at the same time.

He continued in the same vein once they got home. He promptly sent everyone away, even the old woman, and closed the brushwood gate at the entry to the yard, breathing hard as if he was preparing to do something really terrible. Small as he was, the child was seized with a sudden panic. Until now Kim Song-su had never once raised a hand to them, though he often gave them a good lashing with his tongue; he had never felt afraid of him before. At present, however, he seemed to have become another man. As he drove them indoors and followed them still shouting loudly enough for all the neighbours to hear, the two brothers felt quite certain that they were about to be given a really good whipping on the backside.

What happened next was completely unexpected. Once the door to the room was closed and bolted, Kim Song-su suddenly stopped shouting and began to sob. Soon tears were streaming down his cheeks as he gazed at the two brothers.

"Young masters! It's not right! Do you really think you have nothing else to look forward to in life than to grow up as the children of a poor wretch like me? I may only be an ignorant bondsman, but I know what a gentleman's duty is. If you don't study, how will you ever be able to restore your family to its former dignity? Who is going to make amends for the bitter fate his noble Lordship underwent? Who is going to comfort the souls of our young Master and Mistress who left this world so full of chagrin? Young masters, what you are doing is wrong. Just being alive is not all there is to life. I beg you, have some consideration for this old heart of mine; my only wish is to see our former master's family happily restored before I die."

It was the only time in all the three years they spent together that Kim Song-su gave any glimpse of the almost religious hope buried deep in his inmost heart. He himself was scarcely old enough to be able to grasp fully everything that Kim Song-su had said, but at least the sincere devotion underlying his words communicated itself to him. Seen from the perspective of the poet he later became, the occasion may perhaps seem rather mundane, yet that was probably the first time in his life that he realized just how essential it was for him to study.

6

From the moment that he saw Kim Song-su's tears, he strove hard to adjust to the village school, if it was at all possible. The words are really too pretentious, since he was still barely seven years old, but he tried to develop a conscious affinity for study. He set out with a new earnestness to master the primer of Chinese characters, that had so bored him before, and made every effort to show affection for his infinitely disagreeable teacher.

The intention was admirable, but nothing turned out as he had hoped. The schoolmaster, with his goat's beard and mousy eyes, was no less cold than before, while to the other boys he was still merely Kaettong, the former serf's kid. It didn't matter how hard he tried, it made no difference; the wounds in his heart simply grew deeper.

Until one day their father arrived! The father they thought they would never see again suddenly walked into Kim Song-su's yard, with the setting sun at his back! It was early in the autumn, three years after their separation.

"My boys, we can go home! You can once again live in the world as the sons of your real father and mother."

He looked haggard, seeming ten years older than when they had parted; he spoke only after holding the boys to his breast and weeping silently for a time. It was the same as on the evening they had left home, the words were brief, with no lengthy explanations; yet his son felt the fear of death that had been stubbornly lodged somewhere deep inside him suddenly melt and vanish.

Their father had set them beside him and was caressing their backs by turns, as if to show how precious they were, when Kim Song-su rushed in, bellowing like an ox, having heard the news, and fell prostrate before him. The emotion in that encounter between master and servant was no less than that of the reunion of father and sons.

"The king issued a most generous pardon last summer. I was intending to come and fetch the boys then, but my health was not up to it, and I was delayed."

After briefly expressing his thanks to Kim Song-su, he told him quite simply what had happened in the meantime. Kim Song-su was curious and kept asking more questions, snuffling noisily the while, so that the boys were able to learn many things.

They heard how their father and mother had gone into hiding, moving from place to place until they finally settled at Yoju, where they were now living; how their baby brother Pyong-ho was dead, as was their grandmother, who had gone back to her old family home and died broken-hearted; how at last extermination had been avoided thanks to the fact that their grandfather was in the direct line of the Changdong Kims.

Equally moving, as soon as all the news had been told, Kim Song-su produced the deeds to his land that he had received from Su-man and offered them to his former master. Their father's integrity revealed itself in high and cutting tones:

"Not at all, you have amply repaid me by taking care of these children. If there is any giving to be done, I am the one who should be doing it."

A little later he even ordered him to stop treating him as "master" in speaking to him.

"You are a free citizen now. Don't humble yourself so much. After all, I'm merely the survivor of a fallen family . . . I don't know if we shall ever meet again, but from now on we meet as social equals."

Yet how strange are the tricks of fickle memory! Perhaps the return of his father had restored him to a normal childhood state; or the realization that death was no longer pursuing him had broken the tension he had been living under? At any rate, that was the last clear-cut memory he preserved of his time at Koksan. He vaguely recalled that Kim Song-su prevented his father from leaving on the next day, as he was intending, and he also seemed to have seen him wrap something up and offer it to his father who again refused to take it, but it was all like a remote dream, nothing more.

He retained no particular memory of what road they took as they walked to Yoju. The only thing he recalled was a fleeting moment as they were passing beside a mountain, when his brother noticed a flaming red maple and asked the name of the place. His father's reply passed into the memory's slow processes of recall and only rose to the surface much later:

"This is Kuwol San, the Mountain of the Ninth Moon, in Hwanghae Province."

7

At this point it may be helpful to summarize briefly what befell his family during those years, in the terms in which society at large has recorded them.

When he was four years old his grandfather, Kim Ik-sun, who was in charge of the garrison at Sonchon, was captured by the rebel army led by Hong Kyong-rae and surrendered to them. That was in the last month of the eleventh year of King Sunjo, 1811. In the first month of the following year, Sonchon was recaptured by government forces and Kim Ik-sun, who had remained in Hong Kyong-rae's camp, was taken prisoner again, this time as a traitor, by the government army.

Kim Ik-sun was transferred to prison and in the third month of that year he was drawn and quartered. During the two years separating his arrest by the government troops and the official measures that spared the family from extermination, they were obliged to live in hiding, dispersed in various localities.

While he was being brought up by Kim Song-su in Koksan, in Hwanghae Province, his parents with his baby brother lived in hiding, first briefly in Yangju and then in Yoju. There must have been some reason for their choice of Yoju, of all places, but none has ever been discovered.

Their father's dream of fetching back the two sons at all costs, so reuniting the family, had arisen after the royal court had ruled that the descendants should not be held accountable for their ancestor's crimes, thanks to the mediation of powerful members of their Changdong Kim family. First their father went to Hwanghae Province and brought him back with his older brother Pyong-ha, but it was no easy affair to raise up again a family that had been once brought down.

It may well be that their father's action in bringing them to Yoju arose from plans he had made for a comeback, basing himself in a place where he was already established. But Yoju was not the kind of place where they could put down lasting roots. In the meantime, the few objects of value that they had been able to take with them on their flight were all gone, and the few family connections they had were no help to the descendants of a traitor.

It looks as though his father had nourished some hopes because he was one of the Changdong Kims, and because he still had property in Seoul. But while the sentence of extermination was lifted, the family estates remained confiscated and the Kims felt no goodwill towards kinsmen who had compromised their political career.

A few months of frequent visits to Seoul had brought their father nothing but the hurt of endless rebuffs and frustrations, so eventually he ceased going there.

Once it became clear that nothing was going as he had hoped, his father resolved to leave Yoju. In order to secure immediate necessities, he had no choice but to go somewhere where he could find help of some kind.

"Let's try Kapyong. I have a few acquaintances there; who knows, perhaps they may help us. If not, I can settle somewhere and do school teaching."

That was what his father said to his mother one day, as he came in from making visits, ignoring the boy's presence. So they left the clear waters of Ipo, before they had spent even one year living beside the ferry-landing there.

8

His hazy path, still so unclear to him, now led towards Kapyong. He was only eight years old, yet already he was experiencing a third change of home. But because this time he set out under the protection of his parents for a destination that was not far away, he preserved no special memories of the move.

It must have been some time in the third or fourth month of the year. His father observed the formal segregation of the sexes and walked some way ahead, while he and his older brother followed on behind with various bundles on their backs, together with their mother who was carrying their newly-born little brother Pyong-du strapped to her back and a large bundle on her head. Their father looked utterly wretched, despite the formal hat and dress he was wearing; already his sickly complexion was obvious.

As he walked on ahead he would stop occasionally, but it seemed that it was because he was having difficulty in breathing, rather than because he was waiting for the three of them to catch him up.

There was just one strange memory of their journey that

remained engraved in his memory even long afterwards; it happened when they had been on the road for about half a day.

They were on an uphill path that ran alongside a stream; just where a steep climb began the boys and their mother decided to rest for a moment; they put their bundles down. Their father, who was not carrying anything, walked on swinging his arms then halted silently about halfway up the slope, perhaps realizing that they were not following him. From below, having got his breath back and wiped the sweat from his face, he happened to look up at his father.

It must have been the effect of the late spring haze and the strong breeze that was catching at his coat, for as his father stood there with his hands clasped behind his back, gazing into the stream, he had the impression that he was about to rise into the air. At the same time, possibly on account of the blue sky behind him, the shabby coat seemed to be shining white and incredibly bright.

"Ah, now father's going to fly away!"

He found himself murmuring words to that effect inwardly: perhaps that extraordinary feeling was a form of premonition of his father's imminent death.

Life at Kapyong was grim. Around sunset on the following day they arrived at the place their father had in mind and the family unpacked their belongings in one room of a royal tomb-keeper's isolated hovel. Their mother took from her finger a jade ring, her last remaining piece of jewellery, and exchanged it for rice while he and his brother climbed a hill that was all dusty from the springtime drought to gather firewood.

The forty or so mile walk seemed to have been too much for their father; after two days in bed he got up, his face gaunt and emaciated, and went to pay visits to those people he thought might help them. For five days, he went around the village and its vicinity but apparently he failed to find the friendship and sympathy he had been counting on. Just once, a sturdy farm hand came bringing a sack of barley, saying it was from a royal tombkeeper who lived on the other side of the hill, that was all.

When they were leaving Yoju, their father had said to his wife that if everything else failed, he could always try teaching, but even that proved not to be so easy. He was not yet thirty years old, and with all the memories he still preserved of life as the only son of a powerful family, for whom even the sky was not too high, it was too early to earn a living by work that disgraced aristocrats only turned to as a last resort.

Besides, the old widower who was firmly entrenched at the village school, having nowhere else to go, was determined to drive out occasional competitors at all costs. Memories of this man too must have contributed their share to his later ill-will towards village schoolmasters.

By then, in any case, his father had become so dreadfully haggard that his worsening health must have rendered impossible any thought of making a living as a schoolmaster. For the last few years, he had resisted with the energy that is born of despair, but during that time chronic consumption had been ceaselessly gnawing at his body, until now he had virtually reached the end of the road.

His relief at hearing of the lifting of the death sentence, the relief of hearing that they were no longer being actively pursued, had only served to stimulate the progress of the disease. By the time summer came, he could hardly take care of himself, let alone teach children.

As autumn came, the family experienced briefly some bright, cheerful days. Perhaps as a harvest-time act of kindness, a former acquaintance of their father's, who had been ignoring them, sent over two sacks of rice; he recovered for a moment after suffering all through the summer. For a few days his spirits were high, he kept talking about how he would open a school, and even began to teach the *Elementary Learning* to the two brothers, his first pupils.

Alas, the sun seems to grow larger as it sets, and this was nothing more than the final brief flaming of their father's life while it broke its bonds with this earth. Before even the autumn came to an end the fire went out and it was all over.

Near midnight on the twentieth day of the tenth month, their father coughed up what seemed a gallon of blood and expired in the hovel where they had been staying. That very day he had been called to the house of a local squire named Yun, in the neighbouring village, who was looking for a private tutor, and he had returned home pleasantly drunk.

Once the hurried funeral was over and their father was buried in the cold ground, their mother tried to put down roots in Kapyong, where they had settled. It really seemed she might be able to scrape a living there and bring up her three sons one way or another, if only she could rid herself of her prickly family pride, for they had made some friends in the area who had formed a good opinion of her.

However, there was to be no lasting connection between their family and Kapyong. The old schoolmaster, who had worked so hard to drive their father away, had finally discovered who they were. The rumours the master had begun to spread while their father was still alive were no longer needed, but there was no stopping them now, even if he had wanted to.

The mere words "a traitor's descendants" were enough to strike terror into ignorant countryfolk. The four of them had no choice but to leave the place.

9

"A traitor's descendants" . . . what did those words mean for him as he grew up?

For a while, from the moment he set out for Koksan on Suman's back until the day their father came to fetch them, those words represented the very negation of life itself. Even though he was too young really to understand what death was, night after night he was woken up by nightmares about dying.

Later, for a while the words became almost meaningless, in the period they spent in Yoju and Kapyong, when their parents offered shelter, albeit not a perfect one, and he could regain some measure of childhood simplicity. That was the time when he came to understand that not being denied the right to live and being granted the right to live amounted to one and the same thing.

Nonetheless, by the time they left Kapyong, those words had gradually begun once again to take on something of their old meaning, rather like an ill-omened charm. For slowly he began to sense from his mother's desperate struggle to go on living with her young sons that even though life itself might not be denied them directly, if their living conditions became too difficult then life itself could be imperilled.

The entire retaliatory system against treason was tenacious and thorough, even when it deigned to show a degree of leniency. The royal court might have decided against carrying out the penalty directly, but that by no means meant that the system as such had abandoned its malice towards them.

The ideology of the system, long inculcated through various pedagogical methods, together with the examples of fearful punishment frequently meted out on traitors, had raised people's responses to an almost instinctive level. Not only the classes who shared in the structures and advantages of society, but even those who were the victims of those structures, had been conditioned to shudder instinctively at the very word "traitor" and to consider treason as some kind of deadly disease that could be caught merely by being in the proximity of the descendants of such a person.

If society as a whole thought and felt in that way, inevitably the descendants of traitors who became the targets of those attitudes suffered fatal consequences in their actual lives. Given humanity's gregarious needs, merely being excluded from society could sometimes be a crueller sanction than any direct punishment would have been.

The inertia of the system was also a problem, its inability to come to terms quickly with a decision-maker's act of leniency. The reason was that while those at the top might come to some decision, the lower levels of the administration were often inclined to follow blindly the system's instinct for self-preservation. That mainly manifested itself in an exact execution of the law; but sometimes while externally it seemed that decisions from above were being faithfully followed, in actual fact some kind of invisible sanction was being inflicted. For example, they might withhold from specific people, or only reluctantly grant, things that theoretically the social system guaranteed equally for all, be it material profit or such social benefits as the protection of the law; from the viewpoint of the victims the results could be more dreadful than active deprivation.

Such a retaliation, practised by the whole system, was what

he painfully experienced as he grew up, while moving from Kapyong to Pyongchang, from Pyongchang to Yongwol, then from Yongwol to a village in a remote mountain valley. There was no precise department or law threatening their lives, yet the wretched living conditions that society silently imposed on them were similar in their effects to a direct threat.

Long afterwards, when he was already grown up, he sometimes wondered whether the leniency they had enjoyed – a particular favour indeed for those times, a whole family exempted from an extended death sentence – had not in fact been intended to substitute an indirect and gradually inflicted social death for the immediate physical death demanded by the law.

It was to avoid such a retaliation by the system that their mother took the three brothers to live in remote mountain villages where their origin might perhaps be more easily kept hidden. Yet no matter how they covered their traces, after a few years of life in out-of-the-way hamlets in Kangwon Province someone always found out about their family's history and the negative consequences began again.

This was what happened in Pyongchang. Their mother had no resources except what she could earn by selling her ability to work; she could hope to earn the best income by her needle, and at last a favourable opportunity presented itself. She was employed as a temporary seamstress in the house of a former clerk in the royal library who had retired early and come back to live in his childhood village.

It was three years since they had left Kapyong; for the brothers it was a time of plenty and comfort coming after long months when they had been more often hungry than full, more often shivering with cold than warm and snug. They only had a single room in a farm shed, but during those few months they were never hungry or cold.

Their mother always came home late in the evening, but one day, after she had been working in that family for less than half a year, she arrived back home at noontime.

"If there was a traitor, it was him, your grandfather; he was the one! What wrong have we done? The state let us go on living, so why . . .?"

She came in, sat down on the floor, stretched out her legs, and began to lament bitterly.

He was too young to understand by what channels their family's origin and history could have become known, or for what reason those people were acting so cruelly towards them, even if the husband was a former royal library clerk. It was no mere accident, however, but a clear sign that the system's spirit of revenge had not abated, and the next day, to escape the exactions that might follow, mother and children left the village; their mother was already in the grasp of a virtual persecution complex.

In the village near Chongson where they lived for two years before going to settle in Yongwol, a similar thing happened, even if the details were different. They had headed blindly southwards on leaving Pyongchang, finally unpacking their things in a village of more than forty hearths, surrounded by level fields unusual for a mountain hamlet. It was their mother's choice, based on a calculation that in such a place she would be able to earn a living by odd jobs and sewing.

In that village there lived a vicious landowner, by the name of Master Hong. In his youth he had looked after the horses belonging to the official translator for the royal envoy to Peking; he made a substantial fortune by shady transactions with which he bought some land in that remote mountain village and settled there. But although he lived in a house with a tiled roof big as a whale's back, and proudly displayed the official head-dress that went with the letter of appointment to the title he had purchased for himself, there was no concealing the coarseness of his menial origins.

He had learned all the worst manners of the mandarin class; all the time left after eating and sleeping he used to spend with women; he had one concubine living in the house and two other regular concubines outside.

Yet that selfsame Master Hong began to harass his mother. By then she was well into her thirties, and all that she had been through meant that there was nothing much left of her youthful charms to inspire male ardour. She had grown up in a noble home and married into an illustrious family, so presumably her deeply-rooted dignity was what had awakened the interest of that old rake.

Hong's sallow, wrinkled face remained clearly stamped in his memory; he must often have come hanging round their hovel. No doubt he proposed various enticements to their mother, directly or indirectly; then finally, frustrated in his intentions, he had recourse in an underhand way to the system's habitual practices.

Master Hong casually told the magistrate's clerk of the family's origins, which he had managed to unearth somehow, at the same time informing on them for having cleared a few square yards of hillside woodland to serve as an allotment, as everyone did.

The local clerk was so shaken by the word "traitor" that he seemed to have been scorched by it; he belatedly set in motion once again the system's retaliatory mechanisms, regardless of the royal pardon given years before. The clerk came running, trampled in fury over the little patch on the hill behind the village that his mother and brother had cleared a few months earlier, and screamed reproaches.

"Insolent wretches! A traitor's breed, and yet you dare to go digging up our country's soil?"

Meanwhile, Hong stood sniggering at one side of the field.

The details of events in the period in which he grew up remain obscure, as if shrouded in mist, even in the otherwise entertaining and lively legends about him. That mist should not be confused with the clouds of mystery that later arose from popular affection.

It was not that anything scandalous needed to be concealed; but the only way in which the legends could deal effectively with their struggles against adverse circumstances was to cover the whole matter with an abstract haze and move on, since any such theme must very soon become boring by repetition.

It is best to follow the example of the old stories, with the two episodes already narrated. To put it briefly, his life from early childhood was so full of experiences of alienation and loss of values that it can well be termed a deviation from any norm. It might be added that their frequent moves were originally a means of escape, but moving finally grew into a habit of his soul. Later in life, when the necessity itself no longer existed, the call of the vagrant life kept returning to lure him away.

Certainly the system's stubborn vindictiveness against the traitor grew weaker as time went by. One sign of that can be seen in the fact that during the last years of his childhood they lived openly in the street that also held the Yongwol county offices.

"That's enough hiding away. Let's go and live in a busy street, lost in the crowd. If it's so hard to conceal who we are, we'd be better off in a place where it's easier to earn a living, at least."

Their mother's decision was made with no particular sign of regret on the evening of the day the clerk had ruined their hillside patch. The two brothers silently concurred; he was thirteen by now, while his brother Pyong-ha was fifteen, already a young man.

Sure enough, less than a year after they had moved to the streets of the town, people had already identified them. But this time they did not move away. They were so weary of running, and in any case the world's malice towards them seemed to be diminishing to the point where it could be endured.

The fact that he was able to grow up as he did, in ways not very much different from those of the class into which he had been born, certainly seems to be not unconnected with a dulling of the system's thirst for revenge. While the family continued to be entirely dependent for its survival on the mother's daily labour and needlework, no people like the former library clerk or the magistrate's clerk ever crossed their path again.

10

If we say that he did not diverge so very much from the ways of life habitual to the class to which he originally belonged, that is particularly true as far as education was concerned. His education had begun in his childhood almost as a form of amusement when the family was still enjoying times of prosperity, in the mens' quarters of their house. It had not been interrupted while he was living as the son of Kim Song-su, and it continued even during those hard years when they were constantly on the move, from Yoju to Kapyong, to Pyongchang, then Yongwol.

Education represents a costly investment for an uncertain outcome at any age, and the society of the late Choson Dynasty was no exception. The fees in money or cloth at the village schools which provided primary-level instruction were not cheap, in comparison with the general standard of living of the period, but the charges were even heavier when students reached the higher levels.

At that time there was no institutionalized school system, and almost nothing in the way of reference works for the use of those who might wish to study on their own; people were virtually obliged to rely on human transmission.

It is really nothing short of amazing that in later days his intellectual level was such that he could stand on an equal footing with the best minds of his age, although his life was full of hardship all the time he was growing up.

His intellectual attainments were almost entirely the result of his own efforts. True, there was the early training he had received from his father, and the classes he attended in various schools and Confucian centres; but all the time he spent in that way was less than an ordinary child would have needed to master a single volume of basic history.

He himself would surely have found it hard to explain the secret of his achievement, but to those who come after, who can view the picture objectively, it does not seem so difficult.

He was never able to receive continuous instruction from a good teacher, certainly, and there was no effective system to help him; but among the factors that enabled him to rise to such high levels of attainment, the first that strikes the eye is the whole character of study at that time. Generally speaking, learning in the Choson Dynasty depended less on reasoning powers than on mere knowledge, based as it was on memorization, rather than a systematic course of academic studies. It naturally follows, if we assume that his native talents lay precisely in those directions, that his accomplishments were less astonishing than they might otherwise seem.

One other possible explanation lies in the plentiful free time he enjoyed, far more than we can even begin to conceive of today.

His mother took charge of all his day-to-day needs, although certainly their standard of living was very low; for according to the generally received notions of the age, so long as he had a book in his hands there could be no criticism of the fact that he did nothing to lighten her task. His older brother soon gave up studying and started working to help cover their needs, which meant that he could use his time freely with an even clearer conscience. It helps to take into consideration the way the period's scale of values was distributed.

Generally speaking, for intellectuals of the Choson Dynasty learning was the origin of all values, and equally their sum total. The state examination once successfully passed, learning gave access to power, wealth, and rank; once it was united with character by means of self-cultivation, it might secure one an almost religious veneration.

Learning affected a person's high or low standing, differences between right and wrong were determined by it, it even made all the difference between wealth and want. The final outcome was a perfect model of the kind of system of values that results when a society is constituted solely by ethical obligations and moral principles, unable to make any distinction between the various values.

It was only natural, in so far as he was an intellectual of his time, that he too should be imbued with such a system of values. Yet that alone is surely insufficient to explain his exceptional devotion to study during his formative years. In addition, another element needs to be included, namely those factors originating in his family history.

When a talented young man of privileged social class is deprived for some reason of his position, he has three ways to react.

The first consists in planning active revolt against the system that has done the depriving; the second involves devoting every scrap of talent and energy to obtaining reintegration; the third is to torture oneself and then quickly find a permanent place among the lower classes.

His brother Pyong-ha, two years his senior, chose the third course, living the life of the common people as soon as he was old enough. But Pyong-ha had far more memories of times past than his younger brother, and in the end the pain resulting from his choice was too great for him. After failing to make anything of his life, Pyong-ha died when he was still only twenty-four years old.

Unlike Pyong-ha, he adopted the second solution. Eager to

regain his former social rank, he clung to study as offering the only way to attain it. Any yearning is bound to be stronger and more ardent when its object has been held, then taken away, than when the aim is some new possession. As a result, he was most likely to be different from any ordinary young nobleman of his age dreaming of a rise on the social scale, by the ardour and effort he put into his studies.

His mother's earnest hopes and prayers for him all blend into the family history as factors sustaining his long quest of learning.

"You're the only one left, now. I beg of you, never forget your mother's poor wounded heart."

As soon as he was old enough, Pyong-ha had thrown aside his books and gone out to work in the marketplace; from that moment on, his mother kept urging her younger son to study, letting the tears flow that she normally avoided showing.

In addition she strove to provide everything he might need for his studies, be it books or paper, brushes, and ink, in full measure, working even more doggedly than in the days before his brother had begun to help earn their daily living. Sometimes it meant avoiding his brother's icy sneer.

People sometimes say that women who have suffered a loss of social standing project their desire for social promotion on to their children with particular intensity. Statistics compiled by a foreign writer show how many of the world's great men have come from families where the mother married a man inferior to her in rank or class, which would support such a view. For those mothers, their marriage is an experience of social degradation.

Clearly, when his mother had married there had been no problem of that kind, she being a member of the Yi family from Hampyong. But what she felt so bitterly after her father-in-law's treachery was very clearly a loss of rank; her subsequent longing for a recovery of lost status was no different from any other woman's ardent desire for social promotion.

She had projected her desire on to her husband, but when he died before even reaching thirty, she naturally transferred her ambitions to her sons; as soon as she saw the eldest lapsing into despair and resignation, she fixed her remaining hopes on the gifted second son.

In addition, there are other factors underlying his intellectual achievements, in view of the circumstances in which he grew up. For example, his docile temperament, some kind of inner awakening or unrecorded fateful incident. On the whole what had to be covered has been covered. At least, by the time he reached his coming-of-age, his learning, accumulated over the years in a process whose precise details have not been recorded, was of a very advanced level.

II

At what moment and in what manner did the poet start to grow in him, the outstanding poet that he was ultimately to become?

To trace his early steps as a poet, the first thing to examine will be the contents of the learning he so arduously acquired. The scholarship of the time, centred on what is nowadays called "the Chinese Classics", was a comprehensive discipline of encyclopaedic proportions which included the natural sciences, philosophy, and history. There were also political science, social science, ethics, and aesthetics. In short, all of today's academic disciplines were there under a single name.

Not that every gentleman-scholar was expected to master all those different disciplines. One whose goal in life was to become a scholar would need to acquire encyclopaedic knowledge, but if the goal was to become a government official, only the necessary portions were to be studied, there were well-defined areas for study, with clear limits. With the system of government examinations as the gateway to a public career, one section of the natural sciences belonged to the miscellaneous category in the examination, to which the middle classes had access, while the category of letters and arts was part of the humanities, which was open only to the gentleman class.

In this literary category, the one area that no scholar could neglect was the so-called "study of literature and poetics". In the literary division of the preliminary examination, it was the only subject; it was equally important in the classical division, where candidates needed the help of poetics in order to express their knowledge of the Nine Classics.

Even in the main examination, where ever-increasing weight was given to the Confucian Classics as the Choson Dynasty wore on, poetics remained equally important as the means of expressing knowledge effectively.

Since the social promotion offered by the national examination was the major driving-force behind his pursuit of learning, it follows naturally that he would make every effort to master the skills found in the "study of literature and poetics", where the very first step was the study of poetry.

The fact that he later gained a reputation above any of his contemporaries for his skill in elaborately wrought styles of formal poetry serves to confirm the suggestion that here lies the starting-point of his poetry.

Nevertheless, it would be over-hasty to conclude that such an unforgettable poet was born and grew up entirely on account of a desire for social advancement; in addition there is a risk of confining the variety of poems that he left behind within too narrow a framework.

If he took the path that made him a poet, it may partly have been on account of an artistic temperament in his blood; a remarkable, heaven-sent talent also played a considerable role.

Then again, the hurt resulting from the family downfall that so deeply marked his early years must have had its own not insignificant share in the formation of the poet within him.

The fear of death and the experience of flight had a brutal impact on his unformed consciousness, which remained in part as a kind of instinct latent within him, in part transformed into a sense of futility and casting a dark shadow over his sensitivity; and there was his early life, never being able to put down roots, always having to move from one place to another, while fragmentary memories of former prosperity returned to torment him like so many wounds. His mother, driven by an exaggerated sense of persecution like a wild animal pursued up a blind hillside gully; the wretched conditions of a life in which he always felt as if his very existence was threatened; the shadow of a complicity that ultimately came to seem like a sense of original sin, on account of the way guilt for crime was considered by society to be inherited; with public sentiment for the preservation of the system more like an obsession than simple obedience and the lust for revenge always being revived by the inertia of the lower administration, he eventually came to consider the state and its laws as nothing but latent violence. Their father, virtually absent from the time he began to grow up; his isolation from boys of his own age caused by their frequent shifts of lodging and his studies outside the institutions, and finally, mingled with all those factors, the many resulting experiences of loss of value . . .

All these elements may not be absolutely necessary to make someone a poet, but must have played no small role as stimuli urging one sensitive soul along the pathways of poetry. Or perhaps, more than that, all his memories from early on that had to be expressed were growing inside him, waiting to find a form of poetry that would aesthetically transform and structure them.

Certain people feel that there is a difference between the kind of poetry he learned and cultivated as part of his studies and that which he left behind him when he was roaming the country as a poet in later times. It might be possible to suggest a distinction whereby the former approximated to a means, to utility, while the later works can be seen as corresponding to an end – art.

Ever since the "Songs of the Great T'ang" of King Yao and the "Songs of the South Wind" by King Shun, poetry has been vested with the function of inculcating good customs and correcting wrong behaviour. As a result, the poetry studied as part of general education always had clear aspects of means and utility, whether it was seen as a necessary part of a reader's studies, or as a leisure activity for a gentleman, or a way of obtaining high marks in the state examinations.

However, poetry soon began to break the ancient bridle and run free, from the great innovators of the Chien-an and Zhengshi Eras onwards, refusing to be restricted within the old solemn forms, be it philosophical poetry of "literal meaning" or moralistic "thoughts without vice", as it passed on down through the Chin, T'ang and Sung Dynasties. The decorative style of Western Chin or the mystical works of Eastern Chin are cases in point, to say nothing of the T'ang's search for beauty, or the plainness that the Sung poets pursued. The preference for the more popular five- or seven-character line over the classical four-character line, seems to have something to do with the same tendency.

Examination poetry was not free of these influences. Its original aim was no doubt to serve political ends or further the practical purposes of the ruling class, but those immersing themselves in it got far more pleasure out of T'ang poetry than from the *Book of Odes*. Consequently, while he trained in the conventions of examination poetry, it would be false to affirm that he was confined within a hidebound, narrowly exegetical line of poetry.

Considering how his learning was mostly done away from institutions such as village schools or Confucian centres, the assumption that his poetry developed with equal freedom becomes perfectly tenable. Progressive aristocratic poets or poets of the Practical Learning, as well as poets from among the enlightened common people, and a host of nameless wandering poets, may all have been good masters for him.

12

Poetry is the product of a consciousness, so the pursuit of a poet may in the end turn out to be the pursuit of a consciousness. However, since that consciousness exists in numerous forms, it is neither possible nor absolutely necessary to comprehend it all at once.

The main concern here is to gain a sense of the consciousness of his age, which underwent various transformations to give rise to his poems. What relationship exists between his own individual consciousness and the ideology of his times, especially that of the ruling system?

He was born and grew up in an age when new ideas, especially the Practical Learning and Catholicism, were being introduced from China. There was no challenge to the monarchy or the system of government as such, but questions were beginning to arise in structural terms about such issues as the possession and distribution of wealth and the nature of human relationships.

Perhaps, if he had simply been able to grow up as the scion of a powerful family, he might have manifested an interest in this new spirit of his age as an enlightened aristocrat. If the stubborn deviations he later manifested towards society and family can be considered as a form of passion, perhaps that same passion might in any case have led him to doubt the ideology of the system.

Unfortunately, though, he belonged to a family that was eliminated from the higher strata of society for treason. It is certainly possible to imagine cases where such a fact would give rise to an even stronger sense of revolt.

It is actually very difficult, however, to find instances in the annals of a stagnant agricultural society where one generation's revolt is passed on to the next and gives birth to another rebellion. Instances are far more common where people have ensured their survival by adhering completely to the system's ideology, dreaming of a reintegration into the social rank they have been expelled from; as already suggested, he was one such case.

Having received the system's permission to go on living as a great favour, his father had then died striving to regain a place within it, while his mother's only wish in life was for a return to their former rank; his parents' influence must have been considerable, and as he grew up he submitted almost unresistingly to the established ideology. Loyalty to the king, piety towards one's parents: scion as he was of a disgraced family that had undergone a grim baptism of death for its failure to observe one of the two, and driven at the same time by an impatient yearning for restoration, that dusty old ideology, handed down through long centuries virtually unchanged, must have struck him as something almost fresh and new.

In addition, he accepted loyalty and piety as a unity; even if he had occasion to think of them separately, he never perceived any conflict or tension between them. For there existed a subtle logic, devised by the absolute despots of Asia and perfected by their lackeys over long centuries. The ruler was identified with the parents. The result was a state ideology that ensured without difficulty the people's loyalty, even when the royal heir was a fool. Incompetent, unjust, what to do? Parents are parents!

All of which notwithstanding, the ruling system of the Choson Dynasty seems not to have closed its eyes completely to the conflicts between the two. Not without a degree of opposition, piety at the family level seems to have been accepted to some degree as having the higher position, not only in the mind of the public but even at an official level. For example, in the case of the crime of non-denunciation, crimes committed by parents were excluded from those cases where denunciation was otherwise obligatory.

In cases of high treason the children were executed with their parents, not because they had failed to denounce them, but as a direct result of the country's having once adopted the law of the Chin by which family responsibility extended over three generations. The great admiral Yi Sun Shin quit a battle on which the nation's whole destiny depended in order to attend his mother's funeral, and no one criticized him.

Some people consider that such a system of priorities derives from neo-Confucian ethics; others acclaim it as the ethical norm of a governing system. If once the two principles of state and family loyalty come into direct confrontation within an individual, such a system of priorities can make the haemorrhage in that person's conscience all the deeper and more deadly.

13

Ever since humanity first discovered the form of expression termed poetry, love has been its most frequent subject; the romantic itinerary often forms the most colourful portion of a poet's biography. Taking into account the systems and customs of the age in which he lived, no great expectations should be entertained, but it is sure to be helpful to pause for a moment and see what women meant to him in his growth as a poet.

As the family moved from one place to another, he sometimes encountered girls who made a profound impression on him. There was the youngest daughter of that tombkeeper at Kapyong, in the outer wing of whose house they spent a summer; and there had been a girl by the well as they passed through the village of Pyongchang: their eyes met and although he never saw her again, her pure cool gaze brought a mysterious pain and longing to his heart for several years after. Then, once they moved to Yongwol, there were chance encounters with various daughters of the marketplace.

Yet it does not seem that there are any painful memories or special images of the eternal female from his youth that can be compared with the fascinating episodes dating from the later years when he was roaming the countryside as a poet. This is mainly due to the general atmosphere of the times.

It was a time when the sexes were strictly segregated from the age of six, not only among the upper classes but even among the common people, as a rule that could not be broken. There were, certainly, stories of young men and women falling in love, as in the tale of Chunhyang or various other regional legends, but these were almost always fictional or otherwise rare exceptions.

It was an age, then, in which encounters between men and women were restricted; in addition, with their frequent changes of residence, the family hardly had a chance to strike up close relationships with any neighbours so that it was scarcely possible for him to expect any such exception.

Admittedly, once they were settled in the town of Yongwol the situation changed somewhat. The merchants and craftsmen in the busy streets were less bothered about keeping the sexes apart, and some of the more outgoing among their daughters made eyes at him in secret, kept smiling at him provocatively, or could be seen hanging around near him. But that was at a time when his feelings made him unreceptive.

The main factor that made him ignore those girls was the longing for social promotion, which was beginning to burn in him with particular intensity at that time. Once his brother had taken the path of a commoner's existence, the whole responsibility for a restoration of the family fortunes fell on him and that in turn drove him to bury himself in his books, the only way to attain that goal.

His particular sensitivity about his social rank equally formed a solid wall between him and the daughters of low-class families.

Physically speaking, there was no great difference between his life and that of his low-class neighbours; his mind, though, was already living on the social level that he was sure he would recover in time to come. As a result, no matter how pretty a girl might be, if she belonged to a social class lower than his own he refused to tolerate any mingling of rank.

His marriage, when he was already nineteen, with a girl from the poor but once noble Hwang family, is not unrelated to that same concern. The reason that he was so very late in marrying, by the standards of the period, was that he kept rejecting easily available brides from lower-class families.

Perhaps the extravagant affairs with low-class women that he indulged in after he had begun his deviant life in later years were some kind of unconscious compensation for the way he had spent his youth. It seems as if he belatedly hurled himself into those indiscriminate sexual adventures only after his ardent hopes of social promotion had been thoroughly doused and the fastidiousness of his youth had lost all its meaning.

14

At last this pursuit of his life through all its deviations has reached the point where the traditional accounts normally begin: that dramatic first episode, involving a poetry-writing contest that he is supposed to have entered and won with a controversial poem.

This is how the legend goes: when he was nineteen, he entered a poetry contest held in Yongwol County and was awarded first prize. The topic set was a comparison between the loyalty of a certain Chong who died resisting the rebel army led by Hong Kyong-rae and the crime of a certain Kim who surrendered to the rebels; his poem was particularly severe in its condemnation of Kim. Returning home in triumph, he duly learned from his widowed mother that the Kim in question was his own grandfather; unable to master the shock, he quit his home and from that day on covered his face with a broad bamboo hat, spending the rest of his life as a wandering vagabond. Considering himself unloyal since descended from a traitor, and unfilial for having called his own grandfather a criminal cursed by heaven, he never again exposed his face to the light of the sun, as a sign that a criminal such as he had no right to walk on the face of the earth.

For a popular tale it is certainly admirably constructed. At first sight, the dramatic reversal seems plausible and the reason offered for his later wanderings appears highly convincing. However, as is clear from what has so far been seen, there is a great difference between the legend and his real life.

It is true that in the autumn of the twenty-sixth year of the reign of King Sunjo, 1826, the year in which he turned nineteen, a poetry competition was organized in one county of Kangwon Province, though it was not Yongwol, and it is true that he took part in it.

At that time, thanks to his brother's decision to abandon study and devote himself entirely to earning a living, the family was in a more settled situation than they had ever known before, while his own studies were advancing towards maturity. He decided to enter that competition as a test of the level he had reached before sitting for the preliminary examination.

However, the facts of the case differ from the contents of the legend from the moment that the subject of the poem to be composed was posted at the competition site.

"Write in celebration of the loyal death of Chong Shi, the county magistrate of Kasan, deploring the terrible crime of Kim Ik-sun." Chong Shi, the magistrate of Kasan named here, was widely revered by the scholars of the time for his loyalty, having perished heroically on the battlefield while resisting the rebel army led by Hong Kyong-rae.

The main problem arising here concerns his knowledge of the Kim Ik-sun who was set up as the contrasting example to Chong Shi. The legend maintains that when he read the subject proposed for the competition, and even after he had completed his poem, he had no idea at all that Kim Ik-sun was his own grandfather. But as has already been seen, the disaster in question occurred when he was already nearly five years old, and it had such an impact on him that it would surely have been hard to forget completely, even for someone with a poor memory. Considering how remarkably sensitive he was, it flies in the face of reason to claim that he had been given absolutely no explanation of why his father had collapsed and died coughing blood so young, or why his mother and his brothers had been obliged to keep moving from place to place and never settle down, no matter how completely his mother kept silent about those things in later days.

There is also something unconvincing in the way the legend tries to stress certain elements in order to lend extra realism to his personal agony. To think that he knew from the beginning that Kim Ik-sun was his grandfather, so that he was obliged to formulate calmly in his poem the inner conflicts arising out of that awareness, is far more moving than the dramatic twist found in the legend.

From the moment he read the topic posted high on the wall of the main hall where the competition was to be held, until the moment, some hours later, when he took up his brush, wrote, and left the place, he experienced nothing less than a concentrated version of all the torments and tensions that he had been obliged to endure in the course of a whole lifetime.

There occurred within him a resounding clash between the two central values, loyalty and piety, that he had sworn ever to live by; put more concretely, between his desire for social promotion or his hope to regain lost rank on the one hand and, on the other, his sense of moral right, which had been raised to the level of instinct by his concern for the first.

When he recognized the name of his grandfather, his thoughts froze, as if he was about to faint. It was nothing but a topic set for a rural poetry competition, but it served to show him clearly that the system's malevolence had not diminished with the passage of time, and that there were towering walls of social difference blocking his return. There was no guarantee that he would not encounter the same malevolence, the same walls, when he came to take the primary or main state examinations.

"It's still not finished. Perhaps my day will never come at all . . ." he murmured bitterly, finally recovering his wits that had briefly frozen under the impact of indescribably violent emotions. He stood up like someone bewitched and made as if to leave the competition site. Nothing was very clear, but certainly until that moment his conscience had been following the lines laid down by generally held opinion.

Before he could pick up his writing materials, however, an abrupt change occurred in his state of mind. Later the precise order of events became blurred in his memory, but at that moment he seemed mainly to be dominated by the logic of emotion. Suddenly his mother's face loomed before his eyes and her tearful plea rang clearly in his ears: "Alas, you are the only one left. You alone can restore our family's fortunes."

Another powerful argument came into his mind: "How can I walk away from here after so many years of studying? This may only be a rural competition of no great consequence, but once I withdraw, it will be the same at the primary examination, and at the main examination. Our return to the old house in Seoul will remain for ever a hopeless dream . . ."

He recalled his young wife, who had seen him off with a beseeching gaze, saying nothing, and his brother who had come home the day before with a sullen expression and thrown him a string of coins: "I'm a man who soon decided never to look up into a tree he couldn't climb, but you've squandered so many years on this stuff, you'd best give it a try. Only don't count on it too much. Time may have passed to some extent, but are they really going to give you a chance now? If things don't go as you hope, you come straight back here, then you and I can set up a stall or farm some land. If there's a wish that we can't fulfil, it can always be passed on to the next generation. If a ruined family manages to rise again by the third generation, why, that's not so long . . ."

His brother had been a casual labourer, and sometimes sold firewood, then, more recently, he had got interested in peddling and had gained himself quite a reputation in the market as a moderately successful middle-man and broker. When his brother had spoken to him in those terms, he had felt a spasm of inward revolt, but given the way things had turned out, they were more forcible in preventing his abandoning the competition than was his mother's pleading.

He settled stealthily back into his place. This time his thoughts began to develop, guided by the cold light of reason.

The principles of loyalty to the throne, inscribed in the basic forms of society, and of family piety, written in the ethics of consanguinity, were equally essential for all to observe. It would be absurd to establish a priority of one over the other.

There have to be standards for such a priority in each particular case, standards which must establish clearly what is right or wrong. If family piety is put above loyalty to the throne irrespective of right or wrong, the logic of blood-ties reduces men to the level of mere animals . . .

His grandfather's choice had been mistaken, wrong not only in the eyes of the state but of opinion at large, and in the end he had been condemned to perpetual exclusion by society as such.

The moment his grandfather had been sentenced, he had become a non-person, had lost all identity, not merely by the state's legal judgment but equally by society's ethical judgment. Could he then still be considered to exist, even on the basis of a morality founded on consanguinity? Surely not. There too, his grandfather had to be considered not to exist . . . The rough logic seemed to come flooding into his mind in a rush.

Once the direction of his ideas had changed, his mind adjusted and began to work at dazzling speed. His exceptional memory selected materials that could be of service from all his accumulated stocks of knowledge; then his verbal skills, that were no less remarkable than his memory, began to give logical expression to his materials.

Soon, even more reasons why it would be wrong to give up began to strike him. Bit by bit those reasons built themselves up into a positive right to stay there, and finally overwhelmed the general considerations that had made him waver before.

I'm going to write. Not about how family piety is one of the highest values of our present age, not about my grandfather Kim Iksun; I'm going to exercise the right of one generation to dispute the erroneous choices of a previous generation. I will wield the brush of objectivity on our ineradicable past and its disputes. Without more ado, having thus made up his mind, he quietly prepared the ideas for his poem as he ground the ink.

His studies, faithful to the system's ideology, enabled him to begin his first stanza without difficulty:

> Kim Ik-sun, you were a true subject
>   descended through long generations;
> the lord Chong was only a mediocre official.
> Yet you took the features of Li Ling
>   who surrendered to barbarians
> and noble Chong earned a hero's name
>   equal to that of Yue Fei.
> Unable to master his fury, the poet sings a bitter song
>   as he fondles his sword beside the autumn stream.
> Sonchon, the town entrusted to you,
>   had long been defended by generals.
> Surely it was a place you should have defended
>   more righteously than Kasan?

Having written thus far, he began to extol Chong Shi alone in order to reinforce the comparison:

> Lu Zhong-lian was not alone
>   in sustaining the nation of Chou,
> and there were many like Chu-ko Liang
>   to aid the kingdom of Han.
> We had loyal Chong Shi:
>   he strove to keep back the wind with bare hands,
>   and died loyally,
> the old loyal subject of Kasan, whose exalted name
>   will shine bright in the autumn sunshine.
> His spirit will return to the southern tombs
>   to keep company with Yue Fei.
> His bones shall go to the western hills
>   to lie beside those of Boyi and Shuji.

After which, clenching his teeth, he aimed his brush at his grandfather Kim Ik-sun:

That year's tidings from the northwest were too lamentable,
Everyone wondered what family such an official came from.
The answer: from the mighty clan of the Kims of Changdong,
a name ending in "Sun", well known by all in the capital.
Surely such a family had enjoyed
great stock of royal bounty,
duty demanded not to yield before even a million foes.
Did the Chongchon River wash away all the horses
you had formerly led?
Where did you hang up all the strong bows
from the mighty stronghold?
Those selfsame knees
that once had free access to the royal palace
turned northwest and bent before the traitor there.
How will such a soul ever enter the land of the dead?
Kings already dead will be there first.

Tears came to his eyes as he wrote. He took them for tears of righteous indignation but underlying his emotion was the memory of all the unhappy times that he, his parents and his brothers had had to endure on account of his grandfather's wrong choice, feelings of resentment and anger towards the man who had been the cause of it all.

The system's ideology, on which he based his indignation, was perhaps a mere pretext to justify his personal resentment.

Furtively brushing away his tears, he added the concluding lines. Meanwhile his resentment had become more insidious than ever, overwhelming the instinctive resistance of the blood flowing in his veins, to come bursting out in one final blaze. If his grandfather's spirit still had a heart, those lines were like a sword aimed directly at it:

A man who forsook his parents, you betrayed your king.
A single death's too slight.
You deserve ten thousand deaths.
You know full well the code laid down
in the Annals of Confucius.

Dishonourable deed! Inscribed for ever
and transmitted in our nation's chronicles.

He left the main hall that day, after submitting his poem to the supervising official, firmly convinced of having acted rightly. It was the same as he drank wine in a tavern while he awaited the outcome. Devoid of any fear of having violated the moral code, or of the least shadow of guilt, his heart beat high, like a general who waits for news of victory, as he tried to recall the lines of his poem.

True, from time to time he could not help falling into painful moments of self-interrogation. Deny it though he might, could he be so sure that his decision had not been caused by his intense desire for promotion overcoming the morality of family obligations? Was he not trying to sever the ties uniting him with his grandfather by deliberately making things worse than they were, while his real goal was to free himself of that sense of original sin which had haunted him for so long? Worse still, was he not setting out to make a dirty deal with society by selling his ancestor to purchase this indulgence?

However, to all these questions and doubts he found himself able to give a confident reply in the negative. Why, even supposing it were true, who could blame me? I have paid too dearly in life on account of a grandfather whose face I cannot even recall.

Grandfather's spirit passed into me through my father before ever he committed that crime. Yet all my youth has been spoilt on the basis of a supposed blood-tie that cannot be proved and that has never even been verified properly. Naturally I'm entitled to reject all that . . .

What could never have been anticipated, though, was the abrupt change in his feelings when he learned that he been awarded the first prize. He set out for the main hall as twilight was closing in; but on the way, feeling impatient, he asked someone who was coming back from reading the announcement who had won. The man spoke his name straight away, then added as an afterthought: "It was really a very good poem of its kind. Of course, it doesn't matter how sharp it is, a sword can't kill a dead man a second time. Still . . . if he has any descendants around, they must be terribly hurt."

His heart had been secretly throbbing in hope of being the winner, yet at that moment for some unknown reason he felt himself touched by a strange feeling of horror, instead of happiness. The armour of self-rationalizations that he had spent hours putting on had seemed so utterly solid; what was it then that had penetrated it so easily and pierced the poor poet's sensitive heart with such pain?

There would be no noisy street parade in a flowered head-dress as there was for the winners of the national examination, but still there would be some ceremony of encouragement of the kind proper to a local poetry contest. The gentleman-scholars of the place would throw a party to which the winner, together with the first and second runners-up, would be invited to receive congratulations; normally the local magistrate would attend as well.

If he won, his original intention had been to reveal himself boldly, manifesting his talents and learning to the full. That might be the beginning of relationships that he had until then never known, relationships that might serve as a precious springboard for his next step upwards. But that one casual remark made by the local scholar who had told him of his success had completely doused his high spirits.

Just why was not yet clear to him, but he suddenly began to fear questions on his origins, he no longer felt so confident he would be able to expose clearly the logic that had led him to ignore the priority normally given to family piety. He finally decided not to present himself before the jury that evening but instead found a lonely inn and began to drink, because of that sudden change in his feelings.

Ironically, what he had guessed might happen and had tried to avoid befell him in that inn. He was thinking back over the day's decision with an increasing sense of inexplicable dread, perhaps because the excitement he had felt at pitting his skills against so many rivals during the competition was waning, while he was losing his sharp sense of self-interest under the influence of the wine; just then a traveller came in.

"Tell me, young gentleman, did you by any chance participate in today's competition?"

The newcomer came into the room where he had been sitting alone and formulated his question as he plumped himself down at the table with a cheery smile, without waiting to be invited. His dress was not too uncouth, yet he seemed accustomed to travelling.

The fellow looked to be some ten or more years older than himself and he did not feel averse to having someone to talk to, so he was not unwilling to share his table with him despite his limited funds.

Before accepting the bowl of wine that he offered, the traveller stated his name and place of origin. He was called Noh Jin, from the Kwanso region. The confidence needed to identify himself abandoned him and on the spur of the moment he said he was such and such a Kim from Yongwol, giving a false name.

After giving free rein for a while to remarks designed to get himself a free drink, Noh Jin suddenly challenged him: "And tell me, Mr Kim, don't you find today's incident rather strange?"

"What are you talking about?"

"That fellow Kim Pyong-yon who won the competition. Why, they say he still hadn't presented himself before the jury when night fell."

At those words his heart sank for no reason, and he made a great effort to conceal his agitation.

"I suppose some urgent business came up."

"No matter how urgent. Even in a small-town competition, coming first is no easy matter."

After saying that, Noh Jin seemed unsatisfied and added:

"How could such a gifted fellow stay hidden in this godforsaken region, I wonder. You know, I was so eager to see a man with such astonishing gifts that I waited more than two hours just to get a close look at him after the lists went up."

"Did you read his poem, then? Was it so extraordinary?"

"A scholar must not only be good at his own writing, he has to be good at judging the work of others. If you took part in today's competition as you say, Mr Kim, didn't you see the winning poem too?"

After chiding him, Noh Jin emptied a bowl of wine then quietly closed his eyes. He seemed to be about to recite something he had memorized.

The poem that he heard Noh Jin begin to recite after a slight pause was none other than that which he himself had written earlier in the day. With an astonishing show of memory, Noh Jin declaimed the thirty-six lines of that long poem smoothly without omitting a single word.

Among all the emotions a poet may experience in life, one of the highest and most long-lasting must be that which he feels when he hears one of his own works on another person's lips for the first time.

He was no exception, and he listened with hushed breath until Noh Jin had finished. His perplexity and anguish might be great, the happiness he felt at such a confirmation of his achievement was equally considerable.

His recitation over, Noh Jin again indicated his admiration:

"I'm a man who gets his living by composing formal poetry, but I've never come across anything as amazing as that. How shall I put it? It's as if I was watching a group of yokels fooling around and suddenly got a bucket of cold water over my head. You see, it is in perfect accord with the principles governing heaven and Nature, while it touches the cardinal principles of politics and ethics."

"Don't you think you may be giving too much value to some fearless lad determined to show off? The spirit of these formal poems has been handed down through thousands of years in every Chinese kingdom, great and small, after all . . . It must surely not be hard to copy and imitate them?"

"Oh no. The formal poem contains such diversified forms of splendour that it is cherished for ever, displaying as it does the very essence of poetry. One can never be certain, but I believe that in time to come the name of this Kim Pyong-yon will be renowned at every level of society, simply on account of his poetry."

He felt grateful and uneasy, sitting there listening while Noh Jin continued to extol his poem. His views were so utterly unlike those of any ordinary scholar that curiosity of a quite different kind began to awaken in him; curiosity about Noh Jin himself.

"I was another of those who had high ambitions while they

were studying; while I was growing up people would tell me how talented I was. But as I already told you, I come from the northwestern region. That means I'm disqualified from public office; no matter how learned and talented you are, it's all no use, there's nothing you can do. Besides, the national examinations are not what they used to be; I spent ten years frequenting them, with no result, just killing time. Nowadays I sell the great formal poems I write to the sons of rich families. When I'm tired of that, I go roaming the length and breadth of the land, as I'm doing now. I'm getting on in life, so when I get back home this time, I'm thinking of opening a little school to scratch a living . . ."

Such was the plaintive tale Noh Jin produced in response to his questions. The talkative guest of a few minutes before had disappeared, and suddenly he found himself with an unhappy scholar of nearly forty sitting at his table.

It was while Noh Jin was lamenting his misfortunes that his heart began to open. It was partly the effect of the wine, but the way Noh Jin had suffered on account of his northwestern origins awakened in him a sense of comradeship with an intensity that he had never experienced before.

"Just supposing . . . if Kim Ik-sun still had descendants living, what effect do you think that poem would have on them?"

He finally broached the topic that he had been trying so hard to hold back inside him. By now Noh Jin too was quite far gone, so he took the remark blithely without any apparent effort at deep reflection.

"They'd be hurt, of course. But that wouldn't be the poet's fault."

"But what if this Kim Pyong-yon were a descendant of Kim Ik-sun?"

"Such things cannot be. That's going too far, even for a drunken joke!"

Noh Jin spoke out firmly, still influenced by the wine. Such firmness only had the effect of driving him further into a competitive mood, leading him to open his heart even more fully.

"Why not? Kim Ik-sun was a traitor. It's a subject's duty to denounce treason . . ."

"That cannot be. Self-cultivation is the basis of statecraft; loyalty to the monarch cannot be attained except by the practice of the virtues of family piety. Such was the teaching of the Great Sage, Confucius himself."

"If parents take the wrong path, to disobey them is a way of practising piety, surely?"

"There is no such principle. If you're a scholar at all, you must know about the filial piety shown by King Shun. His father, deceived by his stepmother, several times had him thrown into a pit to die; yet did the king ever oppose his father? Not once! No one may judge the rights and wrongs of their parents."

The effect of the wine on Noh Jin vanished as he spoke, and gradually he showed signs of beginning to suspect what the other really meant. But he did not want to stop now. Instead, feeling an inner vehemence, he began to expose the ideas he had been refining all that afternoon.

"Surely there can only be parents if there is first a nation?"

"Not so. Loyalty is directed towards customs and systems while piety is addressed towards persons as such. Human beings came first, customs and systems followed."

"And yet in the end the individual lives under the constraints of the institutions."

With that, he yielded to an agitation he could no longer control. He felt that their discussion had now reached its most important point, perhaps because of some extravagant transformation in his ever-increasing inner tension. It may have been the result of accumulated drunkenness, or it may have been a growing sense of guilt, but suddenly he felt as if Noh Jin had known all along what he had done and had deliberately searched him out in order to demand an explanation, which only fired his excitement further.

That was the end of any calm discussion. After a few more words, Noh Jin's lips clamped shut in amazement and doubt, while his own agitated voice poured on and on like water gushing from a breached dam. He began to explain why the descendants of Kim Ik-sun were entitled to revile their ancestor. Here were all the different feelings that had gone sweeping through his mind like powerful flames before he took up his brush during the competition earlier that day.

Noh Jin gazed at him in mute amazement, listening intently to his words which were filled with pent-up resentment. It was only when a tone of lamentation began to intrude on the anger that Noh Jin asked in amazement, as if it had just dawned on him, "You mean to say that you are . . .?"

"It's true. I am Kim Pyong-yon, the grandson of Kim Ik-sun. Was I not right to compose such a poem?"

At that, Noh Jin's face twisted with a mixture of emotions. His feelings left him no leisure to pay attention to such a change of expression, though, for he had passed beyond excitement and no longer cared what happened. He was too busy pouring out the words that had lain dormant inside him for so long, not just all that day, but ever since he had first begun to be aware of life as a child.

"How can you even begin to imagine the life I have led? Do you realize what it means to be called the descendant of a traitor? Just now you were saying that the individual comes before customs and systems, but you can't possibly know how miserably those of us who are deprived of their protection are forced to live. You can't begin to know how tenacious and insidious a revenge the institution takes against anyone who has once disobeyed . . ."

He began to pour out a whole series of excuses for his unfilial behaviour, furnished now by the logic of his feelings in an order the reverse of that which he had followed during the competition. Unable to perceive how Noh Jin's expression had gradually hardened and that an icy smile had risen to his lips, he was entirely bent on proffering a self-justification that was imperceptibly turning into a whining incantation. Tears began to pour down his cheeks, without his realizing it.

"All right! That's enough! It's too grotesque, I don't want to hear any more!"

Noh Jin had taken up the empty wine bowl then banged it down on the edge of the table, cutting him off in mid-stream. His incantation had been wandering to and fro chaotically between his mother's ardent dreams, his unutterably dismal future prospects, and memories of their former prosperity. He suddenly became aware of something brushing like a chill breeze across his brow and came abruptly to his senses. The Noh Jin sitting there opposite him was no longer the same man as the traveller who had come cadging a drink earlier that evening.

"You've wasted a lot of words trying to vindicate yourself, but now I know why you acted as you did. You betrayed your grandfather so that you could get back as quickly as possible to the good old days, nice food, fine clothes, the lot! If I had to listen to any more I'd be obliged to wash out my ears more thoroughly afterwards, so I prefer to leave now."

Noh Jin had spoken coldly, in a style of superior scorn; he shook out the hems of his coat as he rose. Completely taken aback by this unexpected change, he stared up at Noh Jin. He was not really very tall, yet in some strange way his face seemed to loom far above him.

The effect of what was happening before his very eyes and the full import of Noh Jin's words struck his heart like a blow from an iron cudgel. Meanwhile Noh Jin had pulled on his straw sandals, shouldered his bundle of belongings, and was already on his way out through the brushwood gate of the tavern. As he clutched his breast, that was throbbing with anguish, his eyes took a blank farewell of Noh Jin's retreating back.

As if he could feel the eyes following him, Noh Jin paused just outside the gate, glared up at the night sky thick with stars, and growled something to himself in a clear voice.

"I've been begging drinks like this for more than ten years; in future I must be more careful about who I drink with. The grandfather sold the king to buy his own wretched life; now here's the grandson busy selling his grandfather to buy himself honours. I'd rather drink cow's piss than quench my thirst with such a cunning traitor's wine."

Those words struck him another heavy blow of pain. His breast felt as if it would burst, he clutched it even more tightly. A nauseous lump suddenly rose into his throat. Taken by surprise, he brought it up on to his coat and saw it was a clot of crimson blood.

15

According to the legend, immediately after returning from that competition he left home for good and began a life of wandering. That follows naturally from the claim that he learned the identity of his hitherto unknown grandfather only after he had written his poem, a discovery which filled him with shame and bitterness. As already seen, that is merely an example of one error leading to another.

After Noh Jin's departure he spent the rest of the night in a state of complete drunkenness, then left the inn at dawn. He kept thinking back over what he had done and what Noh Jin had said the previous evening, and although he tried to justify himself, the only result was an ever-increasing sense of shame and guilt.

He reached home at nightfall; his mother and his wife were waiting for him, their faces full of hope. He merely told them that his learning was still insufficient, so he had won nothing, then he went to his room and lay down. The expressions of disappointment that his mother and wife were unable to hide only added to his torment. He did not, however, tell them that he had won the first prize. He had decided to act as if the entire competition, and his poem in particular, had never existed.

Two days later his brother came home with a face bright red from drinking.

"I've just been hearing at the market inn how a scholar from Yongwol called Kim Pyong-yon won first prize at the poetry competition over in Chongson; what does that mean?"

The question took him aback but he managed to reply without flinching.

"I couldn't even finish my poem. I suppose there must have been someone with the same name as mine."

His brother looked sharply at him as if he suspected something, asked a few more questions and then, when he continued to deny everything, stalked out again with an air that said, "I find it hard to believe you."

Once his brother had gone and he was left alone in his room, he began to realize with dread that the affair was going to be far less simple than he had expected. If his name had already been rumoured around, people would probably soon be talking about the contents of the winning poem and then someone would tell how the winner had failed to present himself before the jury.

There were already several people who knew that they were descendants of Kim Ik-sun, so once the rumour got around it was obvious that they would quickly realize that he was the Kim Pyong-yon in question.

Not that everybody would be like Noh Jin, surely, but once the thought struck him, he could no longer stay crouching in his room. Suddenly he heard Noh Jin's icy voice ringing in his ears again, and his heart ached.

Finally, he leapt to his feet and left the house with no clear goal in view. At first he had simply been intending to cool his head in the fresh air and try to collect his thoughts, but soon he found his steps taking him towards the street where the drinking shops were. He wanted to find his brother. Not because he already seemed to have some idea of what was going on, but because in such a moment there was nobody else he could talk to.

His brother was at a card table in the back room of one of the inns in the cattle market. He only found him after enquiring here and there; his brother threw down his cards with an awkward smile and stood up.

"What's wrong with you, then? Coming to look for me in this kind of place . . ."

His face was already dark from drink. In his efforts to fit in among the rough gang of market people, he had been drinking hard for the past several years to give himself the nerve he needed.

His brother purposely wore his shirt gaping open with the sleeves rolled up in an attempt to look tough, but the sight of the pallid skin underneath gave him a sudden shock.

"There was something I wanted your advice about . . ."

"Advice? A scholar like you needs advice from me, a market lout?"

At home, his brother would tease him for his zeal in studying, but to his marketplace companions he boasted of how his younger brother was a scholar.

His brother's response that day seemed less designed to tease him than to show off before all the roughnecks sitting round about him. It was the same when he called boldly for the landlady and gave his orders.

"Clear out the room over there and make sure you prepare your best dishes to go with the drink; here's a gentleman who may come home one day with that crown of flowers you get when you pass the state examination."

Once they were sitting alone in the quiet room, though, the younger brother's eyes filled with an anxiety he could no longer conceal.

He suddenly felt guilty for no apparent reason, and hesitated a while before he began to stammer out what was burdening him. He told how he had really been the winner at the competition, and what had been the contents of his poem, he even found himself repeating what Noh Jin had said.

Perhaps the years spent working in the marketplace had sharpened his brother's insight into human nature, or perhaps he was quicker on the uptake because they had both shared the same fate, in any case his brother understood exactly what was troubling him before he had even finished telling his story.

"Of course, people are quite ready to understand if we bear a hidden grudge towards our ancestors; but if ever we betray those ancestors in the hope of gaining some respect for ourselves, then trouble starts. You're really in a fix. You know the saying, 'A word with no legs goes a thousand leagues?' Once the full story gets around, you're going to have a hard time, no matter what excuses you make. Everybody may not feel the same way as that scholar you met, but still, once public opinion inclines in that direction, people's private sympathies are going to take second place and you'll find it very difficult to stay on here."

The elder brother's expression was bitter as he said this. There was none of the teasing or chiding that was customary with him; indeed, as he went on his words were tinged with a comforting note.

"Loyalty and filial piety may be basic values for scholars, but for people like us they're more like two poised swords. If you cling to family piety, loyalty cuts you, and if you go grovelling after loyalty it's family piety that brings you down. That's why I gave up the whole damned gentleman-scholar thing, it was too much of a headache; but you're bright, I thought you might scrape through somehow. Well, there's no going back on what's done; we'd better think carefully about what to do next."

His brother might force himself to be violent, ready to strangle his vulgar rivals out in the market for a tiny profit, but inwardly he was no ordinary vendor.

Maybe Pyong-ha's drinking, his tenacity, his blustering even, were all ways of filling the gap between his inner self and the physical reality he found himself immersed in. His younger brother had always taken these things as self-inflicted torments, and had disapproved of them, but on hearing him speak now, he felt deeply moved.

The next morning, his brother came to see him with a surprising decision already taken. After the previous day's drinking he had fallen asleep in the afternoon and at dawn was just waking up when his brother arrived; it had been a long time since he had seen him with a face untouched by drink.

"I was thinking about things last night, and I reckon it's time we left this town. Luckily there's a place I'd already been looking at, I think we'd better go and live there. It's about twenty miles from here, not far from Wasok Village in the direction of Uipung; I know a valley up there that will do just fine for the likes of us to live in, hidden away. To tell you the truth, I'm sick and tired of this vendor's life. And I can't stand seeing mother still going out to work for other people now she's getting old . . . One way and another I've managed to save a bit, too, so we can buy a patch of land up there; once it's been cleared and dug it shouldn't be too hard for us all to scrape a living. It'll be a hundred times better than living here with people picking on us all the time."

It was all very sudden, but he agreed with his brother that it was the best thing they could do. Their mother may have felt that something unusual must be afoot, seeing the two brothers whispering together, for she accepted the elder brother's suggestion with no great objections.

So finally, late in the autumn that year, they set out once more for a new home, in what is now Wasok Village in the Hadong district of Yongwol County. Altogether there were six of them: his wife and himself, his older brother Pyong-ha and his wife, his mother, and his younger brother Pyong-du.

16

The year that followed was destined to be a very special period. They settled in a valley called Oduni, a little way outside of Wasok; there they built a small, thatched cottage and began a quite different kind of life from anything they had ever known before. This time it was a farming life, based on the small paddy field they had bought with his brother's savings, and a vegetable patch they cleared on a nearby hillside.

He put away his books and went out to work with his brothers. Inevitably, the various farming tasks, such as transporting loads in an A-frame on his back, which he had never done before, were hard work and left him exhausted; yet he felt more peace of heart than at any other moment.

The sense of satisfaction, the happiness of producing something, everything in his life was new and therefore affected him more intensely. After hoeing the field, a job that felt more like fighting a battle, he would sit there wiping away the sweat and gazing up at the white clouds as they floated across the sky; such moments made his earlier ambitions and dreams seem completely meaningless.

All six members of the family, from his thirteen-year-old brother Pyong-du to his mother, who was not yet fifty, were fit and able to work; as a result they succeeded in gathering a rich harvest. Their well-tended fields produced bigger and better crops than any of their neighbours' and they soon had such a store of firewood, dried plants, mushrooms and wild fruit, that these alone would have been sufficient to keep them from starving during the winter. They were surely the most contented and happy moments of a lifetime, not only for him but for all the members of the family.

Yet that contented and happy time was not destined to last for long. Their mother had renounced nothing of her earlier hopes and prayers, and she it was who brought about the first cracks in their contentment. In the beginning, she had seemed to be readily adapting to the new life, seeing that it had been concerted by the two grown-up sons; but as she gradually realized what it all meant, she began to manifest feelings of resistance.

It was the morning after they had completed their first rice harvest, in the autumn of the year following their arrival. They had cooked some of the new rice and there was soup made from meat bought in the village; as the whole family was sitting at table, his mother addressed him in sorrowful tones.

"Ah, back when we used to hear you reading aloud to yourself in the house, I could relish even thin corn gruel; now here we are eating beef soup with rice, and I just can't savour it at all. Have you really decided to spend the rest of your life like this, working on a farm?"

His mother's words seemed to tear at an old wound inside him.

A similar incident occurred about one month later, when his first son, Hak-kyun, was born. His mother had scarcely had time to express her joy at seeing her first grandson before she heaved a great sigh that he was clearly intended to overhear.

"A boy's been born all right; but what a miserable existence he's going to have! Born in this god-forsaken valley, the son of a farm labourer, it's as clear as river water that he'll grow up no better than an animal."

He himself was too young to have given up all ambition and this factor was no less powerful than his mother's ardent dreams.

Although he had experienced a tremendous shock the previous year, and this new life they had begun was quite unexpectedly attractive, that was not enough to uproot completely the desire for social promotion that had once been so intense in him.

As autumn began, he felt a longing for study come alive again just as he was beginning to experience a sense of uncertainty regarding their newly chosen life.

What is more, even without his mother's remarks, the birth of his first son gave him cause to think about his future.

Everything would not come to an end with his own life, after all; the family line would be handed down from one son to another without interruption, his son had inherited the blood of their grandfather, as he had done, meaning that he in turn would be forced to live under the same yoke, unless someone could free them; and this new life he had embarked on was clearly powerless to set them free. At which point in his reflections, he suddenly started to feel that the self-sufficient life of the past twelve months had been an utter and disgraceful waste of precious time.

The winter months that followed played their part in nudging him back towards his books and his previous aspirations. Snow fell exceptionally early that year, and in such quantities that the paths leading up into the hills and down to the fields were soon blocked; once such days came, with nothing to do but stay indoors, it was almost natural that his books should emerge from the wicker hampers in which they had stayed bundled up for so long, if only to occupy the hours of enforced idleness. There had been a moment of hesitation before he took out the first volume; once that was out, the next quickly followed, until in no time at all his books had recovered the place in his life they occupied when he was studying before; and with them came, one by one, the ambitions that he had nourished back in those earlier days.

The first person to perceive this change was his wife, since they lived in such proximity. Now his wife, belonging as she did to the Hwangs of Changsu, had never had to undergo the loss of rank and fortunes that his mother had suffered as one of the Yi's of Hampyong. When she was born, her family had already fallen almost to the level of the humblest classes as a result of events several generations earlier. Since he was still a gentleman by birth, their marriage had rather brought her up a few rungs on the social ladder. Perhaps it is not surprising, then, that such a woman could never really understand the ardent dreams of a woman of her mother-in-law's background, nor even the fierce desire for social promotion that her newly-wed husband had displayed in the early days of their marriage.

Her own dreams were no different from those of any other village girl, she only wanted to have a large number of children without having to worry about where the next meal was coming from, and to live happily with her husband.

For such a young woman, the year they had just spent together as a simple farming couple must have been the happiest in her life.

Unlike the previous year, when he had been straining to keep up the deportment and dignity of a gentleman-scholar, it was only now that she experienced what conjugal affection might mean; she also appreciated a life in which they lacked less and less. At present the way she had spent the first months of their marriage struck her as having been vain and foolish; she had worn herself out looking after him, jumping every time he happened to glance at her or clear his throat, abashed by her husband's incomprehensible obsession with a security that depended on obtaining something, although it was not clear exactly what, full as he was of ambitious dreams.

Even if such a woman could not share deeply in his life, nobody was better placed to be aware of the changes happening in him.

On the day when he first drew his manuscript copy of the *Literary Anthology* from the dust-covered wicker basket, she gazed at him with a heart full of misgivings she could not understand and asked: "Will you try again . . . to be a scholar?"

"No, I just thought I'd fill the idle hours with some poetry."

He had smiled awkwardly as he answered, then the other books came out one after another, and he began to change.

She would fall asleep in the evenings leaving him poring over a book, then wake to the sound of repeated sighs and find him sitting with the book closed, sunk deep in thought.

His elder brother had likewise become aware of signs of a change in him, once the light in his room began to stay burning late into the night. But by that time his brother was sick. Perhaps he had caught their father's consumption, or maybe the hard work of the previous summer had finally ruined his health, that had never been very good, coming as it did on top of several years of hard living and hard drinking in the marketplace; from early autumn that year his brother began to spend more days lying sick in bed than up walking around in good health, exactly like their father at the same age. Pyong-ha's spirit suddenly weakened, too, and he began to turn to his younger brother for support as he had never done before.

"You know, you're the only one I can count on. It looks as though you'll have to take charge of the household."

Even when they were discussing quite minor questions his brother would simply tell him: "I'm sick. You decide what's best," and suddenly look sad; he was certainly in no state to scold or prevent him, even though he did not like what he was doing. He often simply watched him from a distance, sometimes with eyes full of the same misgivings as his wife's, sometimes with what seemed a deliberately heightened air of expectancy.

The last person in the family to realize that he had plunged back into his books, and that his desire for social advancement was gradually rekindling, was his mother. She was only too glad to welcome the change in him.

"Of course! That's the way! We're not the kind of family that can be content to remain mere peasants. Why, by now your second cousins probably have gold and jade beads of rank dangling from their hats. On my side of the family there's one of your age who's already passed the minor exam and one the primary. Study with all your might, rise to high office, and set your mother free of her life's burden of bitterness."

As she spoke those words she seemed young and spirited again, quite unlike someone who was already a grandmother.

Meanwhile, the winter deepened.

His brother's sickness and his wife's misgivings grew correspondingly deeper. But his mother's hopes and his own tenacity burned with ever-increasing fire.

17

The long winter at the end of 1827 passed and the spring of the new year came. His elder brother, who had alarmed them all by coughing up blood on three occasions during the winter months, seemed to gain new energy once the warm spring winds were blowing and was soon up and about again. It was as if he had never been ill, and he displayed an unprecedented determination in getting everything ready to resume work in the fields, sorting through the seeds and turning over the manure.

In retrospect it was clear that in doing so Pyong-ha had been squeezing out the very last drops of his diminishing strength.

His brother too was not the man he had been the year before. He showed no sign of going out to work in the fields, but instead told his wife to prepare his things for a long journey; by now her misgivings had turned into acute apprehension.

The second part of the preliminary state examination was due to be held that year, which was a special year for such examinations, so it might be assumed that he left home and went up to Seoul in order to take the exam. There are obstacles to such an interpretation, however. According to the generally accepted story of his life, he ought by now to have been roaming in the Diamond Mountains; there is also no record or oral tradition to the effect that he ever passed the first part of the preliminary examination, without which he would not have been qualified to take the second part.

There is one weighty opinion to the effect that we may infer from his exceptional talents that he had already taken the first part of the exam, since he was now twenty-one.

If this is the case, it follows that he might indeed have gone up to Seoul to take the examination. However, another opinion stresses the absence of any record or report to support this, and considers that he merely used the examination as a pretext for going to Seoul. Obviously, these two theories diverge widely as far as their contents are concerned; yet it is hardly necessary for us to be over-concerned about which is correct. No matter which opinion one adopts, it makes no difference to what follows in the story. For, quite simply, he did not take the examination that year.

Some may still be wondering by what kind of reasoning he managed to spur himself on and rekindle the fires of social ambition.

After all, the events of two years before, the poetry competition and the traumatic encounter with Noh Jin, the scholar from Kwanso, had been of enormous consequence, and not only for himself, since they had forced his brother to change his job and driven the whole family into virtual seclusion. Yet it may be that this problem too does not demand over-detailed investigation. The various reasons that may have caused him to change his mind have already been discussed, and the rest can be roughly conjectured from the grim intensity he manifested in his quest for the restoration of his rank during the two years he spent in Seoul. Besides which, the things people do in their lives are not always founded on processes of strict logic.

Likewise there is no need to linger over the reactions of the family when he announced that he felt obliged to go up to Seoul to take the state examination. Naturally his mother was glad; his simple wife felt troubled because it seemed to her that her husband was being taken away from her for good by this cursed dream of high office; his older brother sent him off with a blessing although he did not approve, for his will and body had both been weakened by sickness; his four-month-old son Hak-kyun showed his utter ignorance by a few meaningless burbling noises.

His brother Pyong-ha's eyes filled with tears as he took his leave, perhaps because he realized that it might well be their last farewell.

Having said goodbye to his family, he left behind him the valley in which he had lived happily for a while, and set off into the springtime where flowers were just beginning to bloom.

The wings of his soul, that had been drawn in tightly during the long winter months, once again stretched wide towards the outside world. But they were not yet the wings of a poet.

18

It may sound very odd to people who are accustomed to the old legends about him, if now they are told that after going up to Seoul for the state examination, he spent more than two years staying as a house guest with a powerful man named Ahn Ung-su.

Yet in a volume entitled *Haejang Anthology*, a collection of works by Shin Sok-wu who was one of Ahn Ung-su's literary associates, there is quite a long piece entitled "The Story of Kim

Tae-rip", which seems clearly to be about him; there are a few points of contention, but even those who query the identification generally accept that he is indeed the subject of the story. Perhaps the makers of the traditional tales omitted this portion of his life because the impression they had of him, based mainly on his later life as a poet, did not correspond at all with this picture of a man in quest of a government career, currying favour with the high and mighty and living as their house guest.

What, then, of his plans to take the examination?

He certainly went to the examination site, either because he wanted to see what it was like after his previous experience, or because he really did intend to take the examination. What he discovered there, though, was the true state of the examination system, infinitely more rotten and corrupt than rumours had suggested, certainly not a gateway opening on to high office in fulfilment of his obsession with regaining a place in society.

To begin with, there was no way a poor scholar just up from the country like him could ever secure himself a place to take the exam.

The candidates were very numerous, and because it was important to occupy a good place, it made all the difference between success and failure whether one submitted one's roll of paper for the examination early or late; all the best places were occupied since the night before by servants sent in by the sons of powerful families. These would occupy wide areas, spreading mats and even circling them with stakes; if anyone came near they would glare at them and frighten them away.

Their master, the young scion of some mighty family, would only arrive on the following morning, accompanied by a crowd of attendants among whom might be someone to compose the required poem, perhaps even a scribe to write it for him! So the poor, helpless rural scholars, thrust aside by these men's might, had the greatest difficulty squeezing themselves into the farthest corners of the examination area; even if one managed to squeeze in somewhere, his writing paper was scarcely put down before it was buried under a mountain of scrolls belonging to other poor, helpless scholars, and reduced to tatters.

The chaos in the public-examination system was such that even the actual writing of the answer was affected. Plagiarism, books smuggled in and consulted surreptitiously, papers exchanged between candidates, or brought in from outside already written, answers written in advance after gaining prior knowledge of the examination topics: every kind of trickery was used, and all of it hard to practise if you were not the son of a powerful family.

He experienced a mixture of feelings on seeing with his own eyes a state of affairs he had hitherto only heard about. He might with difficulty attain a certain level of learning, it would still be easier to pluck a star from the sky than to regain his former rank by fighting his way through such a pandemonium to pass the examination.

Whether he went really intending to take the exam, or only to look, he was so full of feelings of despair that he made no attempt to put even one foot inside the examination site; he simply saw the scene from a distance, then headed for a nearby tavern. He found it just as crammed full of candidates.

The nearby taverns, naturally, and even those far from the examination site were all crowded with country gentlemen in a situation similar to his own, full of discontent and busily downing drinks though it was still broad daylight. Clearly the reports were true that had said there would be more candidates coming from the countryside for the exam this year than from Seoul itself.

"Look, old friend, you can write better than I can; can't you turn into another Yu Kwang-ok and think up some good plan without dying for it? *[Yu was the main character in a classical novel, who wrote another person's examination answer for money, then committed suicide when the authorities found him out.]* I reckon I'll have to be looking round for a rich family to lean on from now on."

He heard those words just as he had at last managed to squeeze into a corner in the third or fourth tavern he tried.

It was nothing but a conversation between members of a group of young scholars from the countryside who had given up any hope of trying to take the examination; but for some reason he felt as if the words were addressed to him directly. They seemed to be telling him that he would either have to take up hack writing as a profession or wheedle his way into some powerful household as a house guest and wait for his time to come.

Yet when he became a house guest of Ahn Ung-su soon afterwards, it was not the result of abject grovelling, as has generally been imagined. At times he had vaguely thought that even such a course would be better than nothing, but he had never gone hanging around powerful people's houses, and even less had he singled out Ahn Ung-su as someone he might approach. His meeting with Ahn was more like a strange twist of fate, and it is more accurate to say that Ahn Ung-su compelled him to come and stay with him.

Seeing he was already in Seoul, he spent a few days looking around with little enjoyment, then began the long trudge back to Yongwol.

He reached the edge of the river at Dokso after half a day's journey, and found there a group of young scholars on a poetry-writing excursion. The marquee covering them, to say nothing of the lackeys hurrying to and fro with trays and dishes, served to indicate that these were the offspring of influential families.

Spring had fully come; the breeze was balmy and the waters of the river, which had before been chilled by the melting ice, were now warm enough for him to wash his feet without discomfort. The hillsides that rose on the further side were already greening with fresh shoots, while the lower slopes he glimpsed behind him seemed ablaze with the fiery glow of azaleas. Time and place would both have been ideal for a poetry-writing excursion, were it not for the fact that the whole country was in the grip of a spring famine, so that the corpses of people who had starved to death littered the landscape.

He headed towards the group of scholars for a quite simple reason. He had walked a long way that day and he was hoping he might get at least a bowl of wine to quench his thirst. As yet he had had no experience of life on the road, but since this was so obviously a gathering of gentlemen, it seemed unlikely that they would prove ungenerous to one of their ilk.

As so often happens in such circumstances, he found the way blocked by the servants busily in attendance about the marquee.

There is a saying to the effect that the servant holding the horse's bridle has more power than the nobleman riding it, and here the servants tried at first to drive him away like some kind of tramp.

He had already experienced hardships in life, but this was the first time he had encountered such an unfriendly welcome and he was not going to take it lying down. He protested and was about to turn away when one of the group looked up and called across.

"What's going on?"

"He's not begging for rice or soup, Sir, he's asking for wine!" The young servant who had blocked his approach so officiously now raised his voice as if denouncing him. But the voice to which he was replying had been unexpectedly gentle.

"To judge by his clothes, he must be a gentleman. Usher him in!"

This young gentleman was none other than Ahn Ung-su. In those days there was nothing more common than a poor wandering scholar, so that costume was in itself of no significance; and yet, guided perhaps by some kind fate, Ahn Ung-su invited him to join the party. He soon realized, from a sarcastic remark made by one of the other scholars, that it was an extraordinary welcome for a passer-by who had merely approached in the hope of a bowl of wine.

"My, Bok-kyong *[that was Ahn's pen-name]* is being generous again!"

As if in indication of the feelings of the company, Ahn Ung-su excepted, he was given a place in a far corner of the marquee, while the food and drink he was served were clearly of the kind destined for passing travellers.

If he had been then the man he later became, such a level of welcome would have been quite sufficient to content him, but in those days he was still a young and inexperienced scholar.

Reluctantly suppressing a proud urge to kick aside the table and leave, he surveyed the company, with their costly clothing and healthy complexions. It was as he had supposed from his first distant view of them; they were indeed the sons of high-ranking families, and the stubborn sense of his own worth that he had previously been feeling suddenly changed into a fierce desire to challenge them.

One of the party addressed him curtly, as if testing him: "This is a poetry-writing party, you know. You're a scholar too, so won't you compose a poem?"

"Would you prefer it to be in five-character lines, or seven-character lines?"

"As you like."

He had never practised impromptu composition, nor learned to improvise, yet a poem in seven-character lines sprang into his mind without much difficulty, spurred perhaps by pride and a spirit of rivalry.

This river has no red cliffs,
  but riding a boat, the fun's the same.
The place seems near Hsinfeng,
  the wine flows so generously!
In a world like this, there's no clear distinction
  between a hero, and an orator.
Wealth makes you Hsiang Yü, and wine Su Ch'in.

The style was not really appropriate for such an occasion, but it was well-fitted to serve as a weapon against those who had been mocking him. A few of the young men present listened to his poem with expressions of disapproval, but most found it entertaining for a scholars' poetry excursion.

In particular, Ahn Ung-su was glad to see that he had not been mistaken about him, and refused to hear of him leaving. Two brothers who happened to be present, Shin Sok-wu and Shin Sok-hee, came to Ahn's assistance and had no trouble in getting his new guest drunk.

He was certainly in no hurry to return home, so he gradually succumbed to the charm of the company's friendly attitude towards him, to the springtime mood, and the effects of drinking, composing several more poems in the course of the day. Some followed the conventions of such gatherings, some were simply improvisations noted down as they arose. One poem in particular was instrumental in bringing him into Ahn's household, the poem "Looking into Myself, I Sing", with its two stanzas of four seven-character lines:

When I gaze up smiling at the blue sky above,
  I seem to forget the things of the world,
But if I think of the path ahead,
  everything looks so far away.
Living in poverty, all I hear is my wife's chiding;
But as I drink madly,
  the market-women's mockery grows worse.

Watching all those worldly cares
  was like a day when flowers fall;
I regarded my life as a moonlit evening sky.
This is all I get for my life's sins and virtue.
Slowly I realize: blue cloud dreams lie beyond my sphere.

When he recited those lines under a growing intoxication, foretelling and exaggerating his uncertain future prospects, Ahn Ung-su began to question him more closely about his circumstances, with all the compassion proper to the son of such a noble family; for he had sensed from the very beginning this passing stranger's misfortune. Ahn could easily accommodate one extra house guest but, more than that, he really did want to help him by having him near him.

On first edging his way into the party, he had presented himself as Kim Ran (Ran meaning "a little bell"), adding that his pen-name was Yi-myong (meaning "ringing"). Since these were people he would part company with after a bowl of wine, he made up playful names for himself, calling himself "a little bell ringing". The reasons why he subsequently lied about his home and family origins in response to Ahn Ung-su's questions, however, were different from those which led him to conceal his name earlier in the day. Tipsy as he was, he soon sensed that Ahn was asking questions with the thought of helping him by having him near him, so he made up a story about belonging to an insignificant family of local gentry from the town of Kwangju in order to conceal his true origin, that had caused him so much pain. As he had anticipated, once the day's excursion was over, Ahn Ung-su took him into his household. That was the beginning of his time as a house guest.

Certainly, he was not completely innocent of all thought of using whatever powers Ahn might wield as a member of a very powerful family. It was not something he had gone grovelling after, but when the opportunity arose he grasped at it, determined not to let it slip by, holding on to it more firmly, indeed, than others might have done.

He was only a guest, yet the concern that Ahn showed for him was unlike anything that he manifested towards other house guests. The *Haejang Anthology* that was mentioned earlier contains these lines in the "Story of Kim Tae-rip":

> Alas! He had truly astounding talents. Yi-myong was the pen-name of Kim Ran; from time to time my brother and I had occasion to meet him while he was a guest of Bok-kyong (Ahn Ung-su), when we were still young; in those days, Yi-myong was devoting all his energies to competition poetry. His scope was vast and far-reaching, and his skill so exceptional that every one of us looked forward to the time when he would become a great master. In addition to writing in the formal examination style, he also applied himself to the study of the Great Classics, so that day after day you could always hear his voice ringing out as he read, while his hands knew no rest as he copied for himself the *One Hundred Scholars*. He wrote an elegant hand, neat enough to be termed finely written . . .

Obviously, the main aim of this passage is to laud his learning and talents; yet at the same time it gives a glimpse of the kind of activities his position as house guest allowed. In short, he was able to spend the whole day in his room, reading and writing, a privileged guest indeed.

It is not hard to suppose, given the way in which he spent his days, that the fires of ambition and intense desire for social advancement were once again burning bright within him.

He must have thought that, with an extra degree of refinement to his learning and the support of a family as powerful as Ahn's, he might after all be able to envisage success in the state examination.

Yet the report of events contained in the *Haejang Anthology* leaves readers completely in the dark on one major point; it tells almost nothing about the reason why he left Ahn Ung-su's house at the end of two years without any tangible gain. It simply quotes him as blaming the unkind treatment he received from Ahn and Shin Sok-hee after they discovered his humble origins. But that really makes no sense at all.

They had both been told from the very first that he belonged to an insignificant family of local gentry from Kwangju; it seems unreasonable, to say the least, to claim that as the reason for suddenly mistreating and making life unbearable for a guest who over the past two whole years had been valued and cared for.

19

In order to discover the real reasons that compelled him to put an end to his time as a guest in Ahn Ung-su's household, it may be profitable to examine the hidden meanings of his words, rather than what he actually said:

"In my youth, I studied poetry for all I was worth; I went up to Seoul and tried my luck there. I was closely associated with the poets and notable scholars of the time. Ahn 'Bok-kyong' Ung-su and Shin 'Sa-su' Sok-hee were renowned, and I was close to them. They assisted me in many ways and I enjoyed their company. But later, once they learned that I belonged to a modest family from Kwangju, they began to treat me unkindly. In turn, when I saw that they no longer accepted me I realized at once that I could no longer rely on their patronage for my social career. It was a sorrowful and painful experience. In the end it nearly drove me mad; unable to endure the disappointment and misery I was feeling, I decided to follow my own impulses. Yes, Bok-kyong and Sa-su only exacerbated my disease . . ."

In these words, spoken much later to Lee Sang-su, a scholar also known as "Nak-bong", what strikes the reader particularly are the words about "my disease" that "Bok-kyong and Sa-su exacerbated".

Undoubtedly, the disease in question was a psychological one, provoked by his inability to regain his initial rank in society; if

Ahn Ung-su and Shin Sok-hee made it worse, that suggests that he had already been suffering from it. In other words, it is better to say that, while the ambition and fighting spirit that had come struggling back to life were crushed once again by something, the unkindness of the two noblemen increased until he could take no more and had to leave.

That was true. From the moment he became Ahn's guest, he devoted his every last ounce of strength to studying, driven by a new prospect of restoration of his rank, but suffered an extremely bitter setback before two years were over. It all began in a chance encounter with some of his distant relatives of the Chang-dong clan.

When he first learned how much of a short cut to success the backing of a powerful family offered, his thoughts had naturally turned to his grandfather's relatives, who included Kim Cho-sun, the king's father-in-law.

They were not at that time in sole control of the court as they later publicly were, but they were nonetheless one of the most powerful families in the capital. Yet the memory of how deeply his father had resented their heartless attitude, still speaking of it on the day before he died, had always kept him from approaching them.

It seemed most unlikely that they would suddenly begin to overflow with kindness on account of one extra degree of distance.

However, one day Kim Chwa-gun "Ha-ok", the son of the king's father-in-law, happened to visit Ahn Ung-su's house, so at last they met. Ahn summoned him before Kim Chwa-gun, as he always did when he had a visitor, praising his learning and scholarly achievements. Ahn probably thought that it might even prove useful to him.

There in Ahn's reception room, Kim showed no particular interest in him. He merely looked, nodded as such visitors always did, then went away after completing the business that had brought him there.

Kim Chwa-gun was ten years older than himself; at that time he occupied a post of the second rank, mainly granted on account of his birth. Later, he was to serve three times as prime minister and was a central power-broker during the reign of King Ch'ol-jong.

Being of exceptional intelligence and possessing a sharp pair of eyes, Kim Chwa-gun saw at a glance who the man before him really was. Presumably their not so distant blood-relationship played its part. In the presence of Ahn Ung-su, he betrayed nothing, but once home, he sent a steward to summon him. Kim Chwa-gun naturally did this under cover of some business so that Ahn Ung-su would think nothing of it.

"Which are you? Pyong-ha? Or Pyong-yon?"

A trace of apprehension had stirred within him and his blood had run cold as he hesitantly approached the house; the moment he entered the reception parlour where Kim's father himself was sitting in the place of honour, Kim Chwa-gun fired the question at him.

The question was so icy, so incisive, that he never for one moment thought of insisting on the false name he had given to Ahn Ung-su; Kim was truly a terrifying figure.

"I am Pyong-yon."

When he made the inevitable reply, Kim Cho-sun, who had been scrutinizing him silently, suddenly began to shout, trembling with rage to the very tip of his beard.

"What? An ill-mannered scoundrel like you, changing your name and sneaking into a nobleman's guest rooms? Speak up, young wretch, what are you after?"

Fierce as an autumn frost, the voice belied utterly the general report of his character, according to which he was so indulgent that he could never accomplish affairs of state properly. There was no trace of the warmth that might have been expected from a grandfatherly relative.

He remained silent.

"You mean to tell me it was for nothing more than three square meals a day that you've been licking Ahn Ung-su's arse all this time?"

Still he said nothing.

"You rascal! Do you dare consider yourself some kind of gentleman-scholar, for ever talking about propriety and decorum, shame and honour? You? Why, it was only by an immense act of favour on the part of the state that you were spared from sharing your grandfather's fate; how in the world could you dare set foot in the capital or look for anything more? Remove yourself from here at once! If you ever come sneaking around Ahn Bok-kyong's house again, I'll have you arrested and flogged!"

Far more deeply shocking than all that, though, was something that Kim Chwa-gun said to him as he escorted him out; his ears were still burning from the fiery dressing-down he had just received.

"I'm sorry to say this, but you must go back home at once. The court is not ready to accept you. Like Father was saying, go home, live quietly out of sight, and think yourself lucky not to have been executed; at least you can perpetuate your family line. You are only going to hurt people if you persist in your impossible ambitions. You'll hurt yourself, you'll hurt Bok-kyong, you'll hurt our whole clan. Did you really think that an axe through the neck was the only way for people to get hurt?"

As they crossed the garden of the men's quarters, Kim Chwa-gun entreated him once more. His voice had grown gentler than it had been at first and this encouraged him to venture a question:

"Was our grandfather's crime . . . so very terrible, then?"

Kim Chwa-gun stopped, looked at him piercingly, then gently asked:

"Do you think that his only crime was not to have died when he encountered the rebels? To have surrendered to Hong Kyong-rae?"

"Why . . . is there something more?"

"Oh yes, much more. Your grandfather did not simply surrender to the rebels, he took a position in their organization, he even wrote something for them, a manifesto urging the foolish peasantry to join them and rise up together."

"What?"

"Oh, there's more to come. When the tide began to go against them, he returned to the loyalist camp, committing an even more perfidious crime as he did so. He got a certain peasant, one Cho by name, to bring him the head of the rebel's chief-of-staff, Kim Chang-si, promising to give him a thousand copper coins. He tried to deceive the king himself by producing it as if all the credit were his. Do you really believe that the world is foolish enough to offer a government position to the grandson of such a scheming traitor, less than twenty years afterwards?"

He heard nothing more of what was said after that. All the extra details about his grandfather's crime that Kim Chwa-gun had supplied were completely new to him.

He could not be sure if his father had known or not; obviously he would never have told his sons, or their mother. He clutched at his breast, racked with a pain far greater than that which he had experienced four years earlier, when Noh Jin had chided him in that tavern at Chongson. As he tottered out through the main gateway, he heard Kim Chwa-gun call after him, in tones of calculated regret:

"You for your part, and we for ours, we all want this to be an end of it. We don't want people to talk about us in connection with that disgraceful episode ever again . . ."

Had he been the man he was a few years earlier, he would surely have left Ahn Ung-su's house straightaway. But he was twenty-three now, and had tasted what the world had to offer, not only the bitter but the sweet, too. He still ventured to hope for the best, not having as yet had a chance to put his patrons' goodwill to any test.

In addition to Ahn Ung-su, he enjoyed the favourable opinion of Shin Sok-wu and his brother, as well as other sons of high families, all of whom admired his talents and learning. He felt that they might still be ready to help him, that it would perhaps make no difference even if they knew just who he was.

His hopes were in vain. Less than three days after his encounter with Kim Chwa-gun, their attitudes had already begun to change. First, Ahn Ung-su began to act coolly; then Shin Sok-hee and the others withdrew their goodwill. It was clear that Kim Chwa-gun, even without directly revealing his real identity, had fatally influenced them against him.

Soon all their goodwill, that had been diminishing daily, had changed into indirect hostility; then he knew that the last strand of hope that he had desperately been clinging hold of, had finally, mercilessly been cut.

He realized that as a mere house guest he could obtain nothing for himself, even if he had been staying with a family ten times the rank of Ahn Ung-su's.

Finally, two weeks after his meeting with Kim Chwa-gun, he silently tied his belongings together into a bundle and left Ahn Ung-su's house. It was in the sixth month of the year.

Sometimes human emotions undergo strange distortions. This is especially the case where resentment or hatred are involved; so it was, no doubt, with the bitterness he harboured towards Ahn Ung-su and Shin Sok-hee. Judging in rational terms, it seems obvious that he should have felt more resentment towards Kim Chwa-gun; but in actual fact the bitterness he felt towards Ahn and Shin was far greater. And his feelings did not modify with the passage of time. That is what he meant when he blurted out that "Ahn Ung-su and Shin Sok-hee exacerbated my disease."

20

It may well be that his decision to live in ways that would deviate decisively from the norms of the period was taken at about this time, just when his last attempt at social promotion had gone drifting away like so much foam. Indeed, when he hurriedly left Ahn Ung-su's house he had not yet decided that he wanted to go home. At that time there was only one option open to unfortunate intellectuals when everything had failed them, and that was the lonely choice of what was usually called "house-guesting"; he already had a fairly clear idea of what such a life involved and felt quite strongly drawn by it.

However, he belatedly received news that his brother had died and that meant postponing such a choice at least for the time being.

When he left Ahn's house he set out on a round of taverns, intent on drowning his rage and resentment. It was on perhaps the third day that by pure chance he ran into an acquaintance from their years in the streets of Yongwol, from whom he learned that his elder brother had died some six months previously, at the end of the previous year; he had not been informed because no one in his family knew where he was.

He threw aside the cup of wine he was holding and set off for

Oduni without delay. When all was said and done, his brother had had a truly wretched life.

Their ways of expressing it might differ, but the resentment his brother had harboured in his breast to the very end was identical with his own. While he had consumed his bitterness in a fierce desire for restoration, his brother had only turned it against himself, deliberately setting out to destroy his own life.

Above all, he felt bitter about the various kinds of wickedness his brother had needlessly committed in the course of his self-destruction, and the way in which people would, as ever, make them the basis of their final evaluation of his brother's character.

Those rowdy scenes, not all equally necessary, in the days when he was constantly hanging around the streets and marketplace. At the slightest excuse, his brother would grab other merchants by the collar, he had even been known to wield a knife. The drinking that all their neighbours used to shake their heads about. For his brother had begun to drink to punish himself even before his bones were fully set, and once he had drunk he would become noisy and violent.

Then there had been his marriage. Their mother had always striven to maintain at least the basic rules of the clan, even though they had fallen so low, but she had been forced to let her eldest son set up house apart. There had been better possible brides, yet his brother had insisted on marrying the daughter of a blind fortune-teller who was the laughing-stock of the whole town. To say nothing of all those many rash, violent acts which brought a frown even to his brow, obliging him to concur with the general opinion people had of his brother, although at the same time he could to some degree understand what he must be feeling. His brother got free of all that once they moved to Oduni, but unfortunately there was nobody up there who had known his brother previously and who could therefore give his true character a fair assessment.

So in the end his brother would be remembered by most of those who knew him simply as that Yongwol marketplace ruffian, a man who seemed sometimes wild and sometimes downright servile, who was always called "Pyong-ha" in a familiar, slighting way by children and adults alike.

Memories of the many hard and bitter times he had shared with his brother made him shed frequent tears along his homeward way. The twenty years between that winter evening when he was four and his departure from Oduni passed in succession before his eyes, making his heart ache.

> Birds at dusk perch to sleep on a single bough.
> At daybreak one by one each goes its separate way.
> Don't you see? Human life follows selfsame laws.
> What's the use of soaking your sleeves with tears?

He tried to console himself with such old verses but as soon as a new memory of his brother's face loomed up, he could not help bursting into tears again. He hastened on, heedless of nightfall, but on arriving home he found something at least as deeply shocking as his brother's death waiting for him.

His mother, who was approaching fifty by now, had suddenly left the house one day and gone back to her family home at Hongsong in Chungchong Province, leaving a letter for him.

> When a person becomes a daughter-in-law in another family, that entails less the enjoyment of inherited wealth than being entrusted with a duty to maintain that family. Moreover, the maintaining of a family involves not merely the preservation of the bloodline but, most precious of all, the preservation of its honour.
>
> When I married into the Kim clan your family was recognized as one of the highest ranking in the capital. But less than seven years after my marriage came the tragedy of our degradation and two generations in succession died before their due time. Twenty years later, although the cause of our disgrace was an ancestor's misdeed, today the duty of raising up this family has been entrusted to your mother.
>
> But what do we see? Pyong-ha is dead and we are without any news of you, on whom all your mother's hopes reposed. Certainly, Pyong-du and Hak-kyun are still alive, but at nearly sixteen Pyong-du is a yokel unable to read even the first thousand

Chinese characters; as for Hak-kyun, he belongs to the next generation and your mother is too old now to be able to transfer her hopes to such a tiny child. In consequence, your mother has been unable to fulfil her duty.

Now the proper course when a person has failed to fulfil her duty as daughter-in-law is that she should be sent back to her original family; it is wrong to try to indulge one's regrets by arguing that there is no one left to send me away. Therefore, your mother has decided for herself to leave here and return to her former home, begging the spirits of your ancestors to forgive her. Words fail me when I think of the homeward journey, already almost fifty and grey-haired as I am; but since I was unable to do what had to be done, how could I ever presume to join the spirits of the Kim family when I die? All I can still hope is that you quickly attain high rank, effacing your mother's sins, and summon me back into your father's family. There is no other way for us to meet as mother and son, so I beg you to attend closely to my words. If ever you were to come for me empty handed, in foolish filial piety, I would take a knife and fall on it, rather than live to set eyes on you again . . .

Such was the gist of the letter, written in the vernacular alphabet. He read it in a state of utter horror.

He had been about to free himself for ever from half a lifetime's vain pursuit, but now it was as though a hand had firmly seized him once again.

At least, his mother's letter had the effect of making him hesitate for a while before finally deviating from the ways of the world. Unlike when he had left Ahn's house, he now spent nearly a year confined in his old home, apparently planning something again. As a result, he began to show a close concern for his family.

He registered his own first-born son, Hak-kyun, under the name of his elder brother, who had died childless; when his second son, Ik-kyun, was born, he registered him under his own name. It was only when all that was done, that he finally left home. Considering how much his leaving home signified a permanent break with his family and with ordinary life, it is not easy to explain such a concern for the future of his clan. The family was the fundamental unit, the basis of the entire structure of organized society, which suggests that even now he still somewhere retained traces of attachment to his former dreams of promotion or restoration.

No matter how anguished his mother's hopes, the fact of the matter was that what could not be done could not be done. Probe and search though he might, there was no way by which he could penetrate the system or regain admittance to the higher ranks of society; once that was clearly established, he at last put into practice the option of deviating from every norm, that had been tempting him for so long. It was early autumn in the next year, less than a hundred days since Ik-kyun had been born.

It was now, as he prepared to set out, that he put on for the first time the large bamboo hat destined in later times to give him the nickname which replaced his true name completely. He wore it to conceal himself from heaven's gaze, to which he felt that he could no longer expose himself with a clear conscience, on account of the sin of disloyalty to the throne he had inherited with his blood from their grandfather, and the sin against family piety of which he himself had been guilty towards his grandfather, to which had to be added a further sin against piety since he had been unable to fulfil his mother's lifelong hopes.

Perhaps there was yet another feeling of guilt he hoped to hide under that all-covering bamboo shield, that arising from the pity inspired by his wife as she saw him off, trembling with a nameless dread yet never once asking him not to go, with Hak-kyun out playing childish games and little Ik-kyun nothing more than a newborn baby.

21

He had set out. Away from home and kindred, from the past and its wounded, shattered ambitions. But he was still only someone deviating from the norm, not yet fully a poet. Needless to say, he frequently wrote poems, but only as one necessary accomplishment of a scholar or a pastime suitable for a gentleman; their dominant emotion was not essentially poetic, rather was it the sense of resentment and enforced leisure which now replaced the ambition that had previously burned in him.

On careful inspection, it rather seems that even his deviation was not initially something permanent. The conjecture that it might have been of limited duration, with room for a later return, is rendered tenable by the fact that after he left home, the first place he visited was the Diamond Mountains, famous for their scenic beauty. There was the feeling that he was leaving the dust-shrouded world behind him for a time; there was evidently also the idea that once the wounds of his heart had been healed by attaining affinity with Nature, he would return and start something new.

In the legends about his life, he and the Diamond Mountains are inseparably related. During the rest of his life he visited the Diamond Mountains dozens of times, giving rise to a host of anecdotes. There are likewise several written records preserving details about that aspect of his life; in particular, there is this passage in the *Nokcha Anthology* by his contemporary, Hwang Oh, a ruined gentleman-scholar of the time:

> . . . In the middle of the night, he kicked me, asking if I had ever seen the Diamond Mountains. I replied that I had not yet seen the Diamond Mountains, reputedly so fine that they can never be forgotten, even in dreams. Kim the Bamboo Hat stared at me piercingly and said, "I see the Diamond Mountains every year. Sometimes I see them twice in one year, in the spring and again in the autumn."

Judging by such an incident, the Diamond Mountains were not merely the scene of all kinds of strange episodes in his life, they appear to have been nothing less than one of the very birthplaces of his poetic vision.

The anecdotes he left behind in the Diamond Mountains have come down to the world transformed in various ways. Their chronological order is so confused that it is hard to tell which if any of them refers to that first visit. One tale, which has become especially famous on account of its link with his poetry, tells how he made an old monk pull out his teeth after claiming to be the best poet in the Diamond Mountains, but it is only guesswork to say that this happened when he was young, and there are absolutely no grounds for saying it happened when he was visiting the Mountains for the first time. But since it is connected with his poetry, it will be meaningful to relate it here.

The story tells how, when he came across that proud monk in the Diamond Mountains, they agreed to a wager whereby they would continue a poem line by line in succession, and whenever one of them could not go on, he would pull out one of his own teeth. The match ended in less than half a day, with the old monk pulling out with his own hand the small number of teeth he still had left. This may well really have happened, for he had mastered the rhetorical style of poetry required for the government examinations, and excelled in the aesthetic form of parallel couplets; even if the story is exaggerated, the incident to some degree serves to suggest the level of his poetic achievement at that time.

As for the other incidents that happened in the Diamond Mountains, the reporting of them can be left to the colourful legends about him. The main concern here is his life as a poet, not as a buffoon, a philanderer, a beggar, or a sharp tongue. There is just one episode that needs to be told in detail, that involving his encounter with the Old Drunkard. For it was that meeting that finally led him to take the turning that made a poet of him.

22

He met the Old Drunkard at the end of his first visit to the Diamond Mountains, while he was on the way down. He was well aware that a path led directly from Nae-Kumgang, the Inner Diamond peaks, via Wei-Kumgang, the Outer Diamond and Hae-Kumgang, the Sea Diamond, as far as Tongchon, but he decided for various reasons to retrace instead the route that had led him to Piro Peak. He had been so late leaving home that if he took the other road he might be obliged to spend the whole winter in the Kwanbuk region, which had a terrible reputation for being bitterly cold. With his little experience of a wandering life, he did not fancy the idea at all. He had not so far formulated any firm thoughts about never returning home, and money was running out too, which helped him make up his mind.

When he arrived back at the small inn near the foot of the mountain, that he had left not many days before, it was sunset on a late autumn day towards the end of the tenth month. With the end of the season, there were no new visitors coming to the mountains, the inn was deserted. He ordered something to drink from the woman there, who had recognized him, and stretched out on the floor of the empty room. Suddenly he noticed a poem, four lines of seven characters, scrawled on the wall:

Reading books, my hair has turned grey;
in sword-practice, the year's come to an end.
Sky and earth are boundless, my regret is unending.
After madly downing ten gallons of red wine from town,
With bamboo hat on I came to the Diamond Mountains
in the autumn wind.

The brushwork looked familiar. Suddenly it dawned on him that it was a poem he had written himself when he was on his way to the mountains. He had left behind a paper bearing a few characters scrawled in a drunken moment; the landlady must have picked it up and pasted it to the wall after his departure. The first line was rather an exaggeration, seeing he was only twenty-four, but the overall effect was too good for him to have forgotten it like that.

He was about to call the woman and thank her for the care she had shown in saving it and pasting it to the wall, when she came in, carrying a little table with his drink. It was so generously loaded with dishes of wild vegetables that he was obliged to begin by remarking on that.

"The old man out there kept on at me so . . . and there's a pheasant I've got, too, I'll bring it in as soon as it's cooked."

She gestured behind her with her chin, and he saw an elderly man in a plain jacket following behind her, his age not easy to guess at. He had not seen the old man the last time he was there. His face made an unexpectedly eerie impression on him; it was so grey that the individual features failed to stand out clearly. It was as if the skin had been soaked in water and faded by the sun.

"She tells me you're the young scholar who left that poem behind . . . May I sit down?"

He was already in the room before he spoke in a slightly hoarse voice. The old man did not glance in that direction, but it was obvious he was referring to the poem on the wall.

"No good at all . . . good to light the fire with; I don't know how to thank you for not burning it, and giving it such an honoured place, too."

"Oh, it's much better used this way than for lighting fires. Sticking it there means we save the price of papering the wall for a few years. There are far too many people who scribble nonsense all over the walls and dare to call it poetry. I hope that when they see that, it'll stop their scrawling."

The old man gave no sign of positive praise but his hearer still felt he meant to flatter him highly, and was searching for a modest reply when he spoke again, seemingly talking to himself:

"After all, you need a fair amount of skill, just to imitate the Chinaman style!"

That took him down a peg or two. It seemed that what he had taken for praise merely meant that he had managed to imitate the Chinese! The esteem he cherished for himself as a poet since his days as Ahn Ung-su's house guest was already beginning to rebel inwardly.

The old man paid no attention to his feelings. He filled the wine bowl and drained it himself before undertaking to fill it again for the younger man to drink.

"So how was the Mountain?"

The question came out in a casual tone, as he was bemusedly sipping his wine. It sounded as though the man couldn't care less about the reply, but was merely speaking for the sake of saying something, while the style suggested seniority. Again his pride was touched. In a flash his hurt feelings produced a couple of lines of poetry, with which he decided to give that self-important old fellow a taste of his own medicine.

"Well, Sir, since I see you know something about poetry, there is something I would like to ask you, if I may; actually, while I was up in the Diamond Mountains I composed the first two lines of a poem, but I've been racking my mind for days now to find the other two I need to complete it."

"I only asked how the mountain was, and now you suddenly start on about poems . . ."

"I wanted to find a single quatrain that would portray the mountain in all its beauty, but I can't think of a proper turn and conclusion . . ."

His words were overflowing with civility, but they hid a malicious trap. If I provide the introduction and development, they implied, I challenge you to provide the rest. He wanted to pay the man back for daring to suggest that his own poem had been a mere imitation of a Chinese model. The old man may or may not have realized his intention; he replied with a faint smile:

"Right, let's hear your half of the mountain first."

He cleared his throat and began to recite:

> Pine pine, fir fir, crag crag, swirl.
> Stream stream, hill hill, place place, strange.

After he had finished, he tried to hide a complacent smile. He felt intensely satisfied at having been able to express in that short moment so much of the splendour he had been quite unable to put into words during his wanderings up in the hills.

But the change in the old man's appearance was extraordinary. The expression on his face suddenly grew clearer, he remained motionless for a moment, then he sighed as he said:

"Why not? That's enough, there's nothing more to say."

"But there are the clouds and the birds, the hermitages, the monks."

"They're all superfluous."

The old man scrutinized him for a while, then shook his head as he murmured:

“Well I never! All the depth of the *Book of Odes* in you, and so young, too!”

“You are flattering me, Sir. A mere frivolous solecism . . .”

“Not at all. It’s the same principle as when we represent the blossom of peach trees by repeating twice the character for ‘burn’ or the drooping branches of willows by doubling the character for ‘depend’. You’ve brought the entire mountain together with just two pine trees, two fir trees, two crags. You’ve represented the mountain’s twelve thousand peaks and eleven hundred waterfalls by simply writing ‘water’ twice, and ‘mountain’ twice.”

There was a pause.

“Yes, that’s the *Book of Odes*. It’s the same depth as when it expresses the fact that every being in the world is different by combining the characters ‘three’ and ‘different’ . . .”

He shuddered inwardly at the turn things were taking, not because he was being evaluated too highly, but because the old man’s approach to poetry was so far removed from what he had expected.

When the man had come into the room, he had not seemed in any way remarkable. His uncovered topknot and plain dress had not helped, of course, while the way his face seemed bloated and faded at the same time, with its strangely indistinct features, had been far from what he felt a true scholar ought to look like. He had taken him for one of those village scholars who pretends to know a lot or else a reject from the local civil-service examinations who likes to show off to the rural dunces. The way the woman referred to him as “the old man” had only encouraged the same conclusion.

His sudden display of pride, on closer examination, had been inspired by the same negative reaction, so that when the old man said that what he had tried to express in his poem was enough, he had thought himself justified, believing that the real reason was his inability to complete it. It was only when he heard the man commenting so deeply on the poem that his inflated ego had begun to shrink. He suddenly recalled his encounter with the scholar Noh Jin from the Kwanso region in that inn at Chongson some four or five years before.

“I am at a loss for words. In actual fact, that was nothing but a sort of comic poem, composed on the spur of the moment, without any deep thought put into it at all."

"I know. That's why I was so surprised. That kind of thing doesn't come by study; you've got to be born with it."

The old man paused and again scrutinized him closely for a time. Then, abruptly, after downing another bowl of wine, as if struck by a sudden thought, he asked:

"So who are you, then?"

"A mere nameless scholar whose career has been blocked," he replied with increased civility.

"That's not what I meant. I meant your poetry. You must have started off like any other scholar in this country, writing poems in the rhetorical style needed for the government examinations. You've given that up. Why?"

"I venture to say that I've come to see that high office is beyond my reach."

"High office beyond your reach? You're still young, you seem to be very talented, why do you say that?"

Normally, when he reached this point he would conceal the truth about himself, or let his pent-up anger overflow. Strangely enough, though, this time he was able to recount his life's story without doing either. One reason may be that his heart had been unburdened to some extent by his recent wanderings up and down the Inner Diamond valleys, weeping and laughing like a maniac. But equally important was the way he found himself drawn to the old man by some strange sense of affinity.

For the first time ever, he talked about his life's pursuits and setbacks without hiding or exaggerating anything. As he spoke, the old man kept nodding silently. He was puzzled to notice the way the lines of the man's face were becoming clearer as it took on a more lively, pinkish hue, while an intense interest in his words shone in his eyes. Obviously not just the result of drinking, it seemed as though some kind of inner light was transfiguring the man's ageing flesh.

"After I saw that poem you left behind when you went away last time, I realized it was only the outer shell, I wanted to meet the young man with such a sure grip on his poems. And suddenly, here we are. With you, I feel that I can talk about poetry," the old man said, smiling and looking about thirty years younger than before. It was hard to understand the change that had come over the old man: as he talked on, he too had grown increasingly worked up without quite realizing it, his strange feeling had grown more intense. Caught between his own excitement and the strange feeling, for a time he was lost for words, while the old man began to question him in intimate tones, as if talking with a friend of his own age:

"So what is poetry, for you?"

The old man looked ready to agree with absolutely anything he might say.

He did not want to disappoint him, if he could avoid it, but he could not make up things he did not feel or express ideas he did not believe in. For him, poetry was "a means by which those above teach those below, while those below satirize the faults of those above" and at the same time "a way to set out the laws of conjugal life, promote veneration of parents, strengthen family ties, and bring beauty to edification", as well as an art "using metaphors to suggest other similar things, whereby the rise and decline of customs may be observed, each person's inner resources may be refined and improved, while faults in the government of those above may be reproved". Poetry was a guide to what was right and good, the way for a gentleman to gain that name, something with which to polish one's true nature, and express inner thoughts.

"I wonder. Is all that still true of your poetry? Like wearing a high hat or having a topknot, like having precious beads dangling from your hat, and wearing pendants, all just because you're a gentleman, a nobleman, a scholar, a man? Something to slash, like a sword; to thrust, like a spear; to lash, like a whip? Just a way to show off your loyalty or your piety, to prove how righteous you are, how prudent you are, how talented you are, how learned you are?"

"That is what I have mostly heard and learned . . ."

"Do flowers bloom for the king, or birds sing to extol the merits of teachers? Do clouds gather because rulers err, and does rain fall in accordance with their subjects' complaints? Is the sunset beautiful in honour of justice, does the moon shine to celebrate decorum? Is the melancholy of a spring day with petals falling all on account of concern for the nation's wellbeing? Is the sadness of an autumn night with leaves falling only caused by grief for parents?"

"In that case, Sir, what is true poetry in your opinion?"

"True poetry stands solely by its own worth. It doesn't have to grovel before the powerful, it has no need to be cowed in the presence of learning. It doesn't have to keep one eye on the feelings of the rich, it has no need to fear the hatred of the deprived. It is not to be measured with the yardstick of what is right, or weighed only on the scales of what is true. It is self-contained and self-sufficient."

"But people have to live together, they are doomed to be bound by systems and culture. There are people who need to be clothed and fed."

"The poet is precisely someone who transcends that. It's only when all that has been thrown overboard that the true poet is born."

"Then what does he gain in return?"

"Poetry. High rank doesn't come, distinctions don't come, wealth isn't won. But sometimes a single line can replace all three."

"Is there poetry like that?"

"Yes, there is. Before those eager to give themselves airs persuaded agitated fools to accept the division of society into superiors and inferiors, and put a collar on the world with their systems and laws and manners, all poetry was like that. Before silly, agitated poets pierced their own noses and handed the bridle to those who like to give themselves airs."

"You don't mean Lao-tzu and Chuang-tzu? You wouldn't by any chance be invoking a nonexistent past in order to prove that you're right to look for your own dream-world in the future?"

"I do not wish to use the names of the dead. I'm simply relying on my own human nature. Besides, I'm not talking about the whole world, only about my view of poetry."

He was then only twenty-four, far too young to accept such views on poetry. He was only just beginning to deviate from a social structure and its system of values that had wounded him deeply, so that the emotion dominating his poetry was still basically centred on the resulting anger and bitterness. The old man's poetic theories were too much in contradiction with his own professed idea of poetry as a means to a utilitarian end for him to be able to accept them. In spite of the awe and the strange affinity he felt with the old man, he slowly began to rebel again.

"What are people supposed to do with such poetry, then?"

"Small uses are always evident, great uses never. A gimlet is made to pierce holes, a cord is spun to bind things. But there's no easy explanation for why the Creator produced the Universe. Does that mean that the Universe is useless?"

The old man continued to argue forcefully, but from that moment his features began to change back. Slowly the light that had seemed to be shining from the sound rosy flesh faded, the features that had been like those of a pretty child began to blur again. He noticed the change at once, but at first only as a strange feeling without any particular significance. He was too busy defending with youthful zeal the ideas about poetry he had developed.

"Such a great use may be no use. Surely, from the smallest creature to the human being, for each the Universe has various uses, right for one and not for another. Then there is no such thing as a great use for the whole Universe, only small uses for each being contained within it."

"There's a difference between saying that something does not exist, and saying that things cannot be explained. Perhaps the great use of the Universe is simply the sum total of all the small uses?"

"Aren't you making small things so big that in the end they become useless? Make a needle as big as a pestle, it's no use either as needle or as pestle. Chuang-tzu made a bird that was too large to live in the world; the Buddha made goodness so vast that no one knew what to do with it. It seems that you are turning poetry into something so great that it no longer exists."

"Poetry was originally a great thing," replied the old man; "it's those corrupt scholars who came after Kings Yao and Shun, after Confucius and Mencius, who have reduced poetry to the small thing you see today. It's been like this for thousands of years. Once it has been confined by Goodness, fettered by Manners, tied fast by Righteousness, and oppressed by Knowledge, how can those who come afterwards discern the original greatness of poetry? I'm not making small things too big to be useful, I'm taking things that have been shrunk so small that they're useless and trying to make them big enough to use as they were originally meant to be used."

The old man now looked just as he did when he first came into the room, with skin that seemed to have been soaked in water and faded by the sun, and features that were indistinct. The voice, too, again sounded hoarse and weak. Eventually the change produced a strange impression on the younger man, it made his flesh creep.

Perhaps for that reason, he stopped being rebellious and began to ask questions that came straight from the heart. Nightfall was making the room dark, the wine was perhaps affecting his vision and preventing him from seeing properly, he may have received an exaggerated impression of change in a simple face, but he felt that in that short interval of time he had observed in the old man the kind of changes that you normally see in a human face over the course of several dozen years. It suddenly inspired him with a mysterious sense of expectancy for what the old man might say about poetry, and he prompted him:

"I understand. But if poetry is of such great use, those who produce it ought to receive some great gain. Yet the only thing the poet gains is the poem itself."

"A poem gained may be considered a great gain."

"But what is that great gain?"

"Something that makes the poet free, and therefore makes others free."

"What do you mean by being made free?"

"Mind and body casting off their bonds," said the old man.

"You say the mind casts off its bonds . . ."

"It's a matter of seeing the original meaning of all things. The world is full of all kinds of meanings. But our minds are so fettered by the lies and falsehoods they make for themselves, that they cannot see the beauty, goodness, or truth of those meanings. Only a mind that has become free can see such things, and that seeing is also a making. Because what exists, if no one can see it, might just as well not exist at all, but if seeing comes, nonbeing is turned into utter being. Originally a poem is something seen, and although we don't say we see a poem but that we make it, that is what is meant."

"In what way is the body made free in gaining a poem?"

"When that profoundest state is attained, the body escapes from the captivity of forms, the prisons of time, and the fetters of space . . ."

At that point the old man's voice grew even fainter than before. There was a waning, too, in the young poet's expectations. These people who speak needlessly difficult words, distort clear meanings, and make simple, obvious things complicated and ambiguous! Suddenly doubts arose in his mind concerning the old man, perhaps because of his age. Why, his claim that by poetry even the body can be set free of time and space sounded like the dotage of an old windbag of a poet basking in a Zen breeze!

"Then is poetry the Way?" he asked, after a pause, mainly with the intention of confirming his suspicions about the old man.

The old man was gasping as he replied, as if to show that he would have no strength left for any more talking after this.

"So you too . . . you reckon my ideas about poetry are just phantoms borrowed from the head of some half-baked monk? Well, you ask, so I'll tell you. Poetry is not the Way. Like poetry, the Way sees the original meaning of things, but it sees by putting one thing in place of another. Whereas poetry sees things without any change in the way they are. The Way ultimately seeks to transcend this world, while poetry strives to become one with the world in which it remains."

With that he painfully rose to his feet, cutting short any further questioning.

"After all, it seems that our ideas about poetry are very far apart. I have certainly met a real poet in you, but not the friend in true poetry I had hoped I might find, apparently. Still, there's one thing more I want to say. So long as you hold your present ideas about poetry, you'll never get rid of the anger and resentment holed up inside you. At best, the petty rewards your poems bring may help relieve the bitterness for a time, but in the end I'm afraid you'll lose your poetry completely . . ."

Several questions rose in the young man's mind as he heard those words but he could not force him to stay. Seen from behind as he tottered out of the room, the old man somehow looked like the stump of an ancient tree shaking in a cold wind.

He stayed two more days at the inn after that, perhaps because he felt dissatisfied with the outcome of their discussion. The warning the old man had added as a parting shot, although it did not strike him as real, had left a far deeper impression than anything he had said about poetry in general.

During the next two days he managed to drink with the old man a couple of times; he waxed eloquent, he prodded, he jabbed, but the fire seemed to have gone out and he could never get the man to talk about poetry with anything like the first evening's fervour. Now and again he might reply in a desultory fashion, but either he could not retain what he had said or it struck him as completely incomprehensible. He changed his approach and tried to find out something about his earlier life, but there too the only thing he learned was that the old man was generally known as the Old Drunkard.

He became more interested in the Old Drunkard as a man than in his ideas, and tried to satisfy his curiosity by addressing himself to the woman he lived with. But she turned out to be not much better informed. Many years before, in a village several miles further down the mountain, there had been a bad outbreak of typhoid and her young husband had died, she too was sick; just then the Old Drunkard had appeared, he had shrouded and buried the husband's corpse, then nursed her back to life. That had been the start of their relationship. As soon as she had recovered, he had brought her up here and they had opened the inn; that had been the beginning of their life together. But they were unlike any ordinary couple; the Old Drunkard would never let himself be tied down. This time too, he had only been back a couple of weeks after spending three years away somewhere.

"I don't know what he is to me. I suppose we've been together, oh, some twenty years now, but I don't know him at all, I really don't."

She smiled faintly as she spoke. It was not the mystifying smirk of someone trying to hide something.

His premonition that the Old Drunkard might indeed be a real poet came from a different quarter. Not from what the old man himself said, or from what he could learn about him from others, but from something he observed by chance with his own eyes, something almost insignificant.

On the morning of his third day at the inn, he happened to glimpse the Old Drunkard as he was walking down a valley not far from the house. It was a little, nameless valley low on the mountain, the view was utterly beautiful. The old man was sitting on a small outcrop of rock gazing into a small stream where bright red and yellow leaves were drifting past. As he followed the footpath down the valley, he recognized the Old Drunkard and turned towards him. He was leaving, and he had been feeling sorry because when he had tried to say goodbye the old man had not been around.

As he was heading towards him, he happened to glance around at the surrounding landscape and felt a sudden shock. There was such a perfect harmony between the apparently dozing man and the natural scenery in which he was set. Generally, the more beautiful a scene is, the harder it is for a person to find any place in it. The Old Drunkard might have been just a block of mossy rock or a lovely pine tree, he blended so perfectly with the water and stones and trees around him. Indeed, it almost seemed that his presence raised the relatively unremarkable valley to new heights of beauty.

He stood there gazing at the old man, then at the scenery around him, not even daring to breathe. That's the Old Drunkard, he kept reminding himself, staring in his direction. Yet the man and the details of the scenery vanished and instead his head was full of the utterly beautiful valley and its harmony.

That was all. Certainly that moment's emotion deepened the impression left by their conversation on the first evening; still, it was not enough to make him change his mind about leaving. He had a lot of debts to pay and repay the world: debts of glory and humiliation, love and hate, right and wrong. His long-cherished dream of high office had been replaced by anger and bitterness, but those fires too could not be put out with a few sweet words. True, the Old Drunkard's ideas about poetry had from the start exerted a strong fascination for him, but they could hardly be expected to captivate him completely at that point in his life. He was still only twenty-four, it was by no means sure that his present deviation from the norm would preclude all possibility of return.

Yet people generally tend to consider that his encounter with the Old Drunkard marks the starting-point of his career as a full poet. Rather a hasty conclusion, perhaps, but not too unreasonable. He left then, and more than twenty years passed before he met the Old Drunkard again; but from that moment he had within him a strong inkling that there was a possibility for life to be full of poetry as such, and a notion that the true poet is one who has renounced everything.

23

Not all nonconformists are poets. But all poets are nonconformists. Some poets have absolutely none of the usual characteristics of a nonconformist. They are faithful to the normal order of life, laughing at its joys, weeping at its sorrows. Yet they too are nonconformists. For if a person is a poet at all, he is bound to deviate from the norm at least in the use of language. Language can rise to the heavenly realms of high poetry only when it transcends the muddy ground of practicality.

If such acts of deviation are the universal fate and true characteristic of all poets, then he was at every moment a poet, from the time he left home at the age of twenty-four. Whatever the Old Drunkard meant for him, and no matter how great the attraction of the safe normality of daily life, in the end he did not return to his wife and children, and to the routine life of his time.

There is a moving story told by an eyewitness of the moment when his act of deviation was finally decided on. According to this story, on returning from his first visit to the Diamond Mountains he actually came as close to his home as its hedge. It was an early winter evening and the first snowflakes were beginning to fall, the light shining through the paper windows seemed exceptionally bright and warm. From inside he could hear three-year-old Hak-kyun muttering in his sleep, while Ik-kyun was crying, he had just been beginning to smile when he left, and he heard the occasional sighs of his young wife. Standing there, he had a vision of becoming a nameless farmer and he was actually about to push open the brushwood gate to go in, when he hugged himself and emitted a long moan. Then he shuddered, as if struck by some thought, shook his head violently, and turned away.

Just as he was leaving the outskirts of the village, he spat a clot of blood on to the snow, which was already beginning to pile up white on the ground; the villagers never knew what sad, lonely creature had left that blood behind. There is no telling which was the more decisive factor, his failure of nerve before the bleak daily routine of life which had unfolded before his eyes, or the Old Drunkard's suggestions which had begun to affect him; whichever it was, in the end he did not return home.

He wandered from place to place, never settling. In cold weather and hot, come rain come snow, he went about in thin clothing, with a bamboo hat on his head and a bamboo cane in his hand. From the time he first left home until the day he died, his dress never varied. No one knows from what moment he became known as a wandering poet, he was all the time writing poems. That too never varied from the time he first left home until the day he died. Likewise his begging. For most of the time, from the moment he left home at twenty-four until the day he died in some small village down in the southwestern region of Honam, at the age of fifty-six, he begged clothing to wear and food to eat from unfamiliar people in unfamiliar places.

Does that mean, then, that those remaining thirty-two years were a mere accumulation of units of time, always with exactly the same colour and meaning? No. Not at all. Although his attire did not change until the day he died, the soul they wrapped was not always exactly the same. Likewise, he invariably wrote poems, but their meanings varied according to the time they were written, and though in his deviation he moved endlessly through the world's peripheries, the eyes with which he viewed the world varied with time. In other words, his life can be divided into several distinct stages.

Certainly, there are many possible ways of dividing his life into different stages, and as many possible disputes as to which is right or wrong. Some may try to divide his life according to the different geographical areas he visited, others may draw lines at thirty and forty and divide his life according to the decades, while yet others may attempt to make a classification by reference to the various social events of the time. But he was undeniably a poet. Seeing that poetry-writing was the most vital activity for him, it may well be that a division of his life according to the kinds of poetry he wrote will prove to be not too far wrong.

24

If the different stages of his life are divided according to the characteristics of his poetry, the first stage will cover the seven or eight years between the age of about twenty-five, when his wandering really began, and the visit he made to Dabok Village when he was thirty-two. During this period he chiefly moved around such places as Tongchon, Hamhung, Hongwon and Tanchon in Hamkyong Province as well as neighbouring parts of Pyongan Province; regional characteristics seem, however, to have exercised no great influence on his poetry.

The main formal characteristic of his poetry at this time is the classical new form based on the solid rhetoric of the poems written for the government service examinations. Some say that the main pleasure obtained in reading his poems comes from the skill with which he deviated from the norms of classical style, but that is more a hallmark of the poems written later.

He showed no special preference regarding subject matter. He liked to display vigorous, intense emotions and avoided writing on topics that were easily prone to sentimentality or frivolous malice.

The techniques he enjoyed using at this time give prime place to pomp and opulence, not unrelated to the rhetoric of the government service examination style, on which his poetic craft was based. Wit and humour may also be characteristics of his poetry at this time, but what distinguishes this from later periods is the effort he still makes to maintain his dignity as a high-class intellectual.

In the background to these features is his nomadic life in those years. He had become a wanderer but he had not been on the road very long, so naturally for a while he had mainly to rely on the patronage of a few old acquaintances. When he went to visit them, nine times out of ten they turned out to be heads of local government sent down from Seoul, or the sons of local landed gentry he had got to know during his time in the capital.

Cho Un-kyong, the magistrate of Anbyon County who took such good care of him, is a good example. He had come to know Cho vaguely when he was once staying as a guest of Shin Sok-wu; now he made him welcome when he came to visit him. Thanks to the kindness of such people he did not suffer from poverty in the early stages of his nomadic life, and he was able to maintain his former sentiments more or less unscathed.

A second thing that may underlie the characteristics of the poems of this period is the class of the consumers for whom the poems were destined. As we saw above in considering the shape taken by his wandering, he chiefly frequented the rural upper classes or people close to this class, such as *kisaeng* girls, and these formed the main consumers of his poems. Invariably what they liked was the culture of the capital city with its formal clichés; the popular style of poetry that he produced later could not have found congenial ground among them.

The process by which he mastered the poetic craft and also his youth offer other background factors that underlie the characteristics of the poems of this first period. These were precisely the kinds of poetry that he had previously mastered, while his aesthetic sense, which had not yet fully developed, to some extent made him readily content with merely conventional forms of expression and techniques. At the same time in his youthful pride he tried to conceal his true state of beggardom under a cloak of bluff and bluster, which was also not unrelated to the characteristics of his poetry at the time.

Above all, one feature that cannot be omitted from this list of background factors is the weakness of his social consciousness. The bitter frustrations that he had tasted had made him so politically indifferent that he almost intentionally turned his eyes away from the political reality and social situations of his time, and clung instead to his own inner world. As a result, his poems naturally sought their themes in Nature and in subjective emotions, for which the most effective form of expression was bound to be magnificently opulent ornamentation and exaggerated emotion.

It would perhaps be meaningful at this point to look at two poems that exemplify relatively well the main characteristics of this period.

> Hermits' ways are distant as clouds;
> At nightfall a traveller's thoughts grow darker.
> Changed to a crane, the hermit flies off, no knowing where.
> News from Pongnae Mountain is faint in my dreams.

> A *kisaeng* in my young embrace, a fortune seems like straw;
> With a jar of wine in daylight, everything's like clouds.
> Wild geese flying on high follow a river's course;
> Butterflies passing green hills cannot shun the flowers.

Both poems are written in seven-character lines, the first is entitled "Pyoyon Pavilion in Anbyon" and the second "On shunning flowers". The first was written for Cho Un-kyong, who was the magistrate for Anbyon County; the second was composed together with a *kisaeng* girl in Tanchon, the two of them composing alternate lines. Both feel like poems written by some vigorous man of taste, betraying no trace of a vagabond's weariness.

The success he scored with this kind of poetry in the first few years was a surprise even to himself. In the reception rooms of the landed gentry, local magistrates and dignitaries, or very occasionally in the room of a culturally vain *kisaeng*, his youth was consumed in a final blaze of poetry and wine.

Sometimes he assuaged their sense of inferiority with regard to the culture of the capital, sometimes he frankly prostituted his talents to their low cultural tastes, while he spent those few years intoxicated by the cheap admiration and applause he received from such great luminaries, forgetting for a time his own resentment and bitterness.

25

But time flows on and everything changes. No flower stays fresh a hundred days, no guest is welcome for more than ten days; likewise changes took place in his life. He had for a time preserved his dignity by constantly moving from one acquaintance to another, but his status as a house guest began to decline as he was forced to have recourse to the hospitality of the same persons for a second or third time. When people began to realize that this was no distinguished man of talent honouring them just once with a visit, but a mere vagabond who kept coming back again, their admiration for his poems diminished rapidly, their material rewards grew accordingly mean. By the time he passed thirty his life had come to resemble that of a typical vagrant of his times, always on the move and living from what he could beg.

His love affairs with *kisaeng* girls seemed more glamorous than they really were but they always came to an unhappy end. What with the financial patronage of local magistrates and the rich landed gentry, to say nothing of poetry and songs, he had the impression that now at last his lonely wasted youth was being fully compensated for, yet his love affairs were always doomed to fail. There might be exceptions but essentially *kisaengs* were a class who sold sex in exchange for financial reward, which meant that he could never become a serious long-term client of such women. Most of them only kept company with him while his patrons provided financial payments on his behalf, and although one might occasionally give herself to him moved by a kind of cultural vanity, that never lasted.

He for his part did not intend to settle for long in the embraces of any such girls. Yet he could not help feeling desolate when he saw their gates slam cruelly in his face while his affection was not yet over and before the pleasure had abated. He thought he had loved and been loved, but once it was over, the relationship always turned out to have been nothing more than a variety of prostitution while at times, because poetry had been involved it provoked, beyond simple wretchedness, an unbearable sense of disgust.

With age a change occurred in his sentiments. As he entered his thirties he realized that he must give up for ever all thought of being readmitted to the upper circles of society; at once he began to be invaded with scepticism concerning the youthful days he had spent intoxicated with wine and cheap applause. He dreaded the thought of growing old as a cheapskate poet no different from a clown; the lonely wearisome road stretching ineluctably before him now began to look very long indeed.

At last his social consciousness, long imprisoned within the iron walls of his political indifference, began little by little to open its eyes to the outside world. As he became more and more tired of his wandering life, his contacts with the common people grew more numerous, forcing him to feel the tragic nature of that primitive life which he had tried for so long to ignore. The fact that he finally decided to take his place as one of them was no mere hypothesis designed to exaggerate his resentment and bitterness, but rather a clearly formulated anticipation; their life was the prototype of the life he too had to experience. As a result he could not help becoming aware of the many social variables that regulated their lives.

With that came changes in his poetry as well. Irregularities and variations were attempted, themes and technique, too, slowly began to diverge from what they had previously been. After five or six years of always writing the same kind of poems, he grew bored with pursuing preposterous, abstract sentiments far removed from the realities of life.

He was equally tired of the high-class establishment, enslaved in their highbrow cultural tastes, and of the newly rising classes who mistook the acquisition of such a culture for the last step in their own social ascension; he no longer even experienced his former enthusiasm for composing poems in tandem with *kisaeng* girls, which had really been nothing more than a kind of tacky foreplay to sex. He grew disgusted with the way he served to justify the rich life enjoyed by the landed gentry and endorse their ease, by staying in their guest rooms, and began to feel physically sick at the wearisome contact with rural intellectuals who regarded him as a model of high culture, desperately striving as they were to console their own blighted talents.

What most decisively marked the end of the first phase was not so much these inner changes as the visit he made to Pyongan

Province at the very end of the period. He was now thirty-one and as far as Hamkyong Province was concerned, begging seemed the only course open to him, since there was no house left where he was welcome, so he crossed over into Pyongan Province, where a fresh shock awaited him, with the local people's evaluation of Hong Kyong-rae's Insurrection.

The reports he had previously heard about Hong Kyong-rae's revolt said that it had been begun by northwesterners and had been quelled by northwesterners. Undoubtedly, for what had finally vanquished the might of the huge northern division of the rebel army had been a force made up of volunteers and reservists from the northern region of Pyongan Province, including Uiju, while the southern division had been halted by a confederation of officials and local troops from the region around Anju. The government troops dispatched from the capital had only rooted out, with great difficulty, the rebel forces that had been driven into Chongju Castle. They had only succeeded after several months of incredibly hard fighting, despite their comparative superiority in numbers.

He had naturally assumed that the northwesterners' verdict on Hong Kyong-rae would be the same as that of the court, but it was not. Perhaps because the people he met from the start of his travels through Pyongan Province were from the lower classes, unlike those in Hamkyong, he found that for them Hong Kyong-rae was no villain, even if they called him a traitor. They used the word "rebellion" to designate what Hong Kyong-rae had done, but looked as though they only said that because they were obliged to, and when they spoke of the new world he had tried to establish they went so far as to betray signs of secret regret. It was bound to come as a shock to him, for he had always believed that treason was invariably an evil, criminal act.

Not that the people there praised or admired Hong Kyong-rae openly, but they never blamed or abused him either. When people recalled how parents or brothers had been killed before their very eyes they might shed tears of sorrow, but very few ever laid the blame on Hong Kyong-rae, and if they spoke of their wartime sufferings they gave first place to the plundering and brutality of the government troops, rather than to the conscriptions and requisitions by Hong's side. All these things were equally a shock to him, for he had long nurtured deep resentment, not simply against his grandfather but even more against Hong Kyong-rae, to whom he had transferred all his grandfather's guilt.

The longer he stayed in Pyongan Province, the deeper grew the shock, until in the end he became highly sceptical about the existing verdict on his grandfather that he had hitherto accepted unreservedly. If Hong Kyong-rae could be regarded in such a light, it was quite possible to have a different view of his grandfather as well. If that were the case, there might be a way of healing one of the ugliest and cruellest of his wounds, his resentment and bitterness might be elevated from grief over his miserable fate to a feeling of true pride, even if that made no real difference in his life.

So, one year after entering Pyongan Province he went to visit Dabok Village, where Hong Kyong-rae's Insurrection had had its base; that day was destined to be the last day of the first phase of his life as a poet.

26

It was early in the summer of the year in which he turned thirty-two that he went to visit Dabok Village.

It had been put under government surveillance and declared a prohibited area for several years after the Hong Kyong-rae Insurrection had been quelled. Twenty or more years had passed and the surveillance had long since been lifted but people still did not like to go near the place. There were widespread rumours in the neighbouring villages that even in broad daylight you could hear the crying of the restless spirits of those who had been wrongly killed, while at night will-o'-the-wisps bright as bonfire flames went leaping here and there.

He too could not enter the village in a sober state of mind, but for a quite different reason than those local people. The thought of going to the very heart of the highly controversial insurrection, as a result of which his grandfather had been beheaded by an executioner's sword, his young father had died coughing blood, while his fate with that of his entire family had fallen from the clouds to the dust in a flash, meant that he could not enter the village in a normal state. He went to a nearby inn and drank from midday onward, spending all the money he had in his purse. He only topped the rise and walked into the valley of Dabok Village as the sun was setting in the west. He had originally planned to visit the village first, then go on as far as Brushwood Island, on the other side of the river, which the rebel forces had used as their headquarters.

By then the shock Noh Jin had given him had become a painful but valuable memory and his emotional reaction as he entered the valley was simply a vague sense of sadness. Though the other crimes that Kim Chwa-gun had once told him of still rankled deep in his heart, now blood-relationship had filled him with tender affection, and he felt no pain strong enough to cause resentment or hatred.

He climbed the old path up the valley, which looked rougher than it really was on account of the tears welling in his eyes. Perhaps because of all those thoughts, he seemed to hear the cries of the innumerable spirits of the innocent dead ringing in his ears, though the sun was still a hand's breadth above the horizon. Strangely enough, that made his feeling of sorrow grow stronger but without any sense of fear or disgust.

There was nothing left standing in the valley. The fact that the place had once served as the base for a great insurrection could only be conjectured from its particular topography, which made it easy to defend against enemy observation and attack, while a large number of soldiers could drill in the hollow area it enclosed. There was no trace of the gold mine that Yi Hi-jo had set up as a decoy to attract people, nor of the huts that had sheltered the rebels disguised as gold-diggers. Here and there, small mounds covered with grass seemed to mark the site of the huts that had been burned to the ground, that was all.

The sight of Dabok Valley provoked a sense of evanescence that increased his sorrow and as he crouched on one of the grass-covered mounds, that had probably once been a hut sheltering the rebels, he began to cry. As the tears welled up, his sorrow became more intense and he wept loudly.

He wept. He wept for his grandfather's misfortune; he wept for

Hong Kyong-rae's vain dreams and for all those pitiful souls who had followed him and died. He wept too as he looked back over his own bitter life, he wept thinking of the lonely, desolate years still lying ahead of him, for how long he could not tell.

He did not know for how long he had been crying. Suddenly somebody behind him asked:

"Who are you? What are you crying so bitterly for?"

Wiping away the tears from his eyes with the back of his hand, he turned and found a middle-aged man standing there, his shadow stretching long in the setting sun.

He looked sinister, with a long scar cutting across his face from the forehead to the top of the upper lip, while the top of his left sleeve fluttered empty in the wind, the lower half having been torn off below the elbow. Yet he felt that this was no ordinary man, in spite of the eerie feeling he inspired.

"Who are you? Why are you crying there?"

As he found it impossible to stop crying immediately, he could not answer and the middle-aged man repeated his question. He did not seem to have asked just in passing. He hesitated for a little while, then decided to answer his question, taking a hint from the sight of his scar.

"I'm merely a traveller passing by. I was crying at the thought of Marshal Hong's wasted dreams, and grieving for the people who died following him."

A strange expression, difficult to interpret, appeared on the man's face. His two eyes sparkled and the long scar on his face, apparently the result of a slashing knife, twitched, but it was hard to tell whether out of anger or satisfaction.

"No, you're no mere traveller just happening to be passing by this area. Nobody dressed in a scholar's costume would ever come all the way here and weep as you did. Speak truthfully. Who are you?"

It was equally difficult to tell from the authority with which he spoke which side he was on. That authority was of such proportions that it aroused an instinctive caution in him and made him hesitate.

"Don't worry. I was the great Marshal's man myself. Even if you are a government agent, I'm not afraid. If you are not, then tell the truth."

The middle-aged man urged him to answer, making his voice a degree gentler as if he guessed why he was hesitating. He was not sure if it was the effect of the year he had already spent in Pyongan Province, or because he had been secretly hoping to meet such a person, but he felt no fear when the man revealed that he had been one of the Marshal's men, in fact he was glad.

He had long been anxious to find out the hidden sides of Hong Kyong-rae's life, and now his curiosity had been inflamed by all he had drunk. Hoping that he might at last learn the things he longed to know, he told who he was without further hesitation.

"I am called Kim Pyong-yon. The former magistrate of Sonchon, by the name of Ik-sun, was my late grandfather."

A look of utter astonishment appeared on the man's face. His eyes gaped wide for a while and he could not close his mouth; then he drew closer and touched his shoulder with his one remaining hand.

"You mean . . . you're the actual grandson of his Excellency our magistrate? Can it be true?"

He felt a strange thrill at the man's exclamation. He had never met anyone who spoke of his grandfather in such tones and with such an expression. While he tried to wipe away the tears that had suddenly started to flow again, he asked:

"Did you know my grandfather, then?"

"I did. I think I knew him best among our people. From the day he was pulled out of bed half-dressed and forced to surrender the government seal to our deputy marshal, Kim Sa-yong, until he was taken away with the last batch of prisoners. But what about you? Did you know him?"

He felt a vague affection towards him echoing in the voice as the man adopted the familiar tones of an older man addressing his junior. He was still not sure what he ought to say, so he replied, as if to test him:

"Yes, I know about him."

"You mean to say, you know him as a shameful ancestor who betrayed the king and surrendered to rebels; who was beheaded as a traitor and his body quartered?"

The middle-aged man acted as if he were interrogating him,

staring into his face with burning eyes. The question was put in so hostile a tone that he could not answer immediately. He looked at the man in confusion.

"Then . . . is there more I should know?"

He asked this cautiously, after a pause. It was a question to which he expected the reply to be a great roar, but the middle-aged man's reaction was unexpected. He looked at him in silence, then suddenly teardrops began to well out.

"There are many things you are eager to learn. Let's go to my house. You'll be needing a place to spend the night anyway, and I've got things to tell you."

Saying this, the man began tugging at the collar of his coat. The sun had gone down in the meantime, the dusk was deepening.

His house was about four miles away, a hut standing isolated at the edge of a village. He did not seem to have a wife or children; for a while he busied himself steaming some potatoes and going to fetch some rice wine and edibles from the village inn.

They ate the steamed potatoes for supper, and drank a few bowls of wine while the man asked various questions about his life. Then, as the moon rose in the early evening sky, the man began to talk about himself.

"My name is Won Myong-dae. We are natives of Sonchon, we've lived there for generations. My father was a clerk in the magistrate's office and my elder brother the chief of staff, but they are both dead now. I myself had the ambition of making a career on the military side, and trained in martial arts. It was the only choice open to people like us because, as you know, we here in the northwestern region are not given any chance to rise in the civilian administration. In the end it was not the government but Marshal Hong who called me and gave me a job to do. I came to Dabok Village in the summer of the year I was eighteen, while my father and brother agreed to remain in Sonchon and collaborate with us. In the twelfth month of that year I went back to Sonchon in General Kim Sa-yong's Northern Army as his standard-bearer. Later I was sent to fight in the battle of Sasongya under the field commander, until I became reduced to my present condition, and that's how I came to know your grandfather."

"What happened to my grandfather?" he asked with bated breath, putting down his wine bowl. Though he could not remember his grandfather's face, the pull of the blood-tie uniting them could not be denied. Won Myong-dae quietly shut his eyes and began to reminisce.

"Thinking back now, that day our rebel forces attacked the magistrate's office in Sonchon is still so vivid in my mind's eye. That day your grandfather had somehow got wind that Park Song-shin, the military commander at Kwaksan, was conspiring with us, so he arrested him and was planning to send him back to Kwaksan under escort. But our deputy marshal, Kim Sa-yong, rescued General Park along the way, then launched an attack on the magistrate's office at Sonchon and took your grandfather prisoner. When your grandfather surrendered, he must simply have been hoping to save his life. The reason why he did what we told him to do while he was under arrest for a few days on charges of corruption and extortion, was no doubt for the same reason. However, it was different after that. He decided to help us of his own free will, as he told us when he took up our cause and was given an official position in our camp. In those few days he had seen a new heaven and a new earth. The love and solidarity he found among our rebel forces must have been moving for someone like him, who had been brought up in the rich ambience of a high and mighty family, and who had known nothing but a steady rise in his public career. When we comforted the fear-stricken population and fed them with grain from the government storehouses, he said that now he realized what a government official ought to do. He said he was distressed to have treated the common folk like horses and cattle, while he merely advocated love for the people, help for the people, as things buried in outdated texts written by dead men, without knowing the truth of what it was to be born in bondage, not knowing what the resentment and bitterness of the common people really were."

"And did he really write that declaration?"

"Declaration? You mean that text he lent to us? Of course, it was written from the very depths of his heart. It was a fine piece of writing, designed to calm the so-called scholars who were even more agitated at any mention of rebellion than the ignorant common people were and to persuade them to join with us in our righteous cause. Only think. Would it have been a normal thing to give a high position to a former magistrate within a few days of his surrender, even if there had not been many qualified people among us rebels? It was a measure of the truthfulness of his sympathy with our cause, and the value of his assistance."

Won Myong-dae's voice was trembling with excitement, but his guest was feeling more troubled than moved. How was he to understand his grandfather's turning against them again later?

"Why then did he cut off the head of that staff officer, Kim Chang-si? Why did he surrender a second time to the government troops?"

"Before I tell you about that, I must first tell you how I came to survive as I did. I was in Sonchon for a fortnight before I went off to Kwaksan in General Yi Je-cho's battalion. I got wounded like this in the battle of Sasongya in the early days of the first month of the new year. Luckily, my brother happened to be a platoon-leader in the same battle so that I managed to avoid being left there as a corpse. I carry in me a strong sense of remorse for not having died alongside the Great Marshal and the other comrades in Chongju Castle. By the time I had recovered somewhat, hidden in a cave in the hill behind my old house, and could just about move around again, it was already the second month of the year and the castle was under heavy siege. Hence I was not able to see or hear at first hand what your grandfather did. But that wretch Kim Chang-si deserved to die. As a staff officer of our army, he should have entered Chongju Castle; but when things turned against us, he sneaked away. We were fools to have been taken in by his smooth words. I don't know what to say about your grandfather's surrender to the government troops. But I can't forget what he said to me as he held my hand, the last time we met. It's still clear in my memory. I think it must have been the fourteenth day of the first month, because it was the day before I was moved up to the cave. Until then I had been receiving the medical care I needed while staying in the house and he actually came to see me at home. He held my hand, which was burning with fever, and said, 'Myong-dae, you have dedicated your life to a righteous cause, do not torment yourself. If I have an opportunity later to write a chronicle of this revolution, I will remember your name first of all.'

"Of course, his surrender can be seen as just one more defection as the situation grew worse and worse, but I do not think it was. He was doomed to die. The court needed a scapegoat for later generations and he fitted the role perfectly. We caught the heads of three of the towns we took, Kwaksan, Sonchon, and Kasan. Chong Shi, the magistrate of Kasan, was killed resisting us; Yi Yong-sik, the magistrate of Kwaksan, managed to escape and performed services for the government troops in their counter-offensive. Your grandfather was the one who had to die as an example, that ugliest and most shameful of examples, execution. I think that they made him die in disgrace because he had surrendered to save his skin, playing that petty trick with the head of Kim Chang-si rather than die nobly. I reached that conclusion when I saw how the sly and greedy Chong Shi was being elevated to the status of a subject of exemplary loyalty. Yet he was reputedly so corrupt that they said he had stolen land all over Kasan. He was a deadly enemy of our commander, Yi Hi-jo, because he had robbed him of his wife and his property. In a situation like that, how could he dream of saving his life if ever he was taken prisoner by Yi Hi-jo's troops? So of course he put up a desperate fight, since he was doomed to die in any case, and then they called it fidelity and loyalty. The world being what it is, what crimes wouldn't they invent to accuse your grandfather of?"

His visitor's eyes had dried as he listened but now tears began to flow again. A poem of many years before came to his mind, a poem calling his grandfather a criminal not fit to enter heaven and Chong Si a loyal subject on a par with Yue Fei, and his heart began to ache. But more than that he was overwhelmed with joy, as his sense of original sin was lifted. He felt he had entered a completely new world, as he asked:

"What was the nature of the justice which Marshal Hong advocated and the young men of the northwest found under his banner?"

"What we dreamed of was a land without discrimination. No discrimination in land-holding; no discrimination according to the social rank of a person's parents; no discrimination based on a person's occupation; no discrimination depending on the size of a person's wealth. What have four hundred years of corrupt rulers done for our people? What but to pillage, oppress, beat, imprison and kill? How could they so cruelly stamp on the modest hopes of the common folk in that way? We tried to give them new hope. We tried to show them a new world."

"But why did you have to make up those stories of a saint being born or that a hundred thousand cavalrymen were on their way from China?"

He was thinking of a declaration which Hong Kyong-rae's rebel forces were supposed to have distributed. If they were fighting for such great and glorious justice, why did they not reveal their leader's true identity but use ambiguous titles, calling him a saint, and even a god? Why pretend they had the backing of nonexistent foreign troops? But Won Myong-dae's reaction was proud and dignified.

"It was Kim Chang-si's idea, to which our Marshal agreed; it was designed to draw in the simple people. There was no other way. In warfare such tricks can be employed, surely?

"It was never widely known, but if once the revolution had succeeded, we even dreamt of a kind of republic in which there would be no king and the state would be run instead by ministers, after the model of the ancient Zhou Era. We planned to abolish the social distinctions dividing people and redistribute the land equally, so that we could construct a natural state here."

This was something he had never heard before. A republic, with no king, land equally distributed . . . it was frightening to hear, but at the same time it made his heart race for joy. Suddenly Won Myong-dae's voice rose in indignant tones.

"And how did they treat us? Never mind about the other places. Just take the example of Chongju Castle. When the castle fell, it is said that there were three thousand civilians and soldiers inside. The government troops let the women go, and children under the age of nine. Then they cut off two thousand heads in the space of one day. Even people who had offered no resistance were slaughtered like cattle or swine. Just think of it. How can you call them fatherland or government troops? How can you call them king and father? And they have gone on persecuting people like you for nearly thirty years."

That was enough. His grandfather might have seemed a traitor in the eyes of the corrupt regime, but for the poor commoners he had been a far-sighted leader, and that was enough to make the way ahead seem suddenly bright. The two emotional pillars that had sustained him for so long, resentment and bitterness, were no mere matter of idle complaints and grumbling, they were something he could bear with pride, part of the righteous cause for a better world. He might not be able to sing his song aloud, it might have to remain for ever hidden in his heart, what did that matter?

He shed tears of joy for a while, then suddenly knelt before Won Myong-dae in a deep prostration.

"You have told me things of great value, brother. I have the feeling that the resentment I have been harbouring has somehow vanished, although it was almost as high as the heavens. Let's go back to Dabok Village and weep aloud all night long, the two of us as brothers."

That moment marks the start of the second phase of his poetic career.

27

Among the titles that later generations gave him is that of "the people's poet". It may not represent fully all the characteristics of his poetry but it is a good enough designation for one particular period of his poetic career, namely the second phase, mainly spent wandering around in the Kwanso area after his visit to Dabok Village.

During this period he lived as a real wanderer, having given up living on the hospitality of local magistrates or provincial patrons whom he had come to know through various acquaintances. Occasionally, when his path led to them, he might still rely on the rural gentry, but now the circle of his contacts was more often than not the commoners' class.

This change in his way of living was largely due to the change in his sentiments. The righteousness of Hong Kyong-rae's cause, which Won Myong-dae had proved to him, had freed him of his former sense of original sin, and that turned his repressed and twisted sense of grievance into something more aggressive. His grandfather might have been regarded as a traitor by the law and the system, but he was now established as a righteous man in the eyes of truth; this served to transform the bitterness deriving from the alienations he had suffered simply for being the grandson, into a right in his own consciousness. From that time onward, he made no secret of being the grandson of Kim Ik-sun.

Though he might not be able to reveal the reasons to the world, he believed that he had the right to bear a grudge against it, the right to rebuke and abuse, the right to ridicule and to jeer. Then, naturally, that belief moved him away from the side of the corrupt ruling class and their auxiliaries who had so oppressed him, towards the class of those alienated as he was.

Accordingly his poetry also changed. He regarded the forms of his art as part of the system, and therefore attempted daring solecisms and variations on them. He began to disregard entirely the basic rules and metrics of poetry which his time demanded he should observe, sometimes even rejecting the exclusive use of Chinese characters in his compositions and introducing words written in the vernacular alphabet known as *onmun*.

Green pines sparsely stand.
People everywhere exist.
The so-called tottering traveller
a lifelong sweet or sour drinks.

Such seven-character poems that he wrote in these years, using a mixture of Chinese characters and native letters, have been seen by some scholars as a bridge between the Chinese-character poems of the later Choson Dynasty and the songs and new-style poems of the Enlightenment Era. In the eyes of the time, however, they were a great solecism, as he wrote:

I write mixing *onmun* letters with Chinese characters,
Like it or lump it, I don't give a damn!

One can detect in his vehemence, beyond any mere nonconformist caprice, a clear intent to challenge conventions. Even tones and rhyme, the importance of which in the poetry of the period was next to life itself, were not left untouched in his onslaught.

ㄱ the sickle tied at your waist.
ㅇ the ring in the ox's nose.
ㄹ the body you go home and wash,
else ㄷ is the end, a dot and you're dead.

In poems such as this five-character quatrain, Chinese characters are partly replaced by syllables written in the vernacular alphabet that yield the patterns of tone and rhyme; in the following poem, that he is supposed to have addressed in anger to an inhospitable monk, he mixes the two systems, using the same final sound in each line:

All the pillars are red indeed.
The traveller at sunset is hungry indeed.
This temple's welcome is grim indeed.
The place for you is hell indeed.

To this period belong most of his unconventional poems, those in which he plays with homonyms and double meanings, or writes Chinese characters with sounds which mean something quite different in the vernacular.

Along with the changes in form, the contents of his poems changed too, in contrast to those of the first stage. In subject matter, he now avoided abstract and preposterous topics, the exaggerated expression of private feeling, for example, or the beauty of nature, or supernatural mountain hermits. Instead, he brought into his poems the tyrannical governors who topped the social scale, then continued on down through the levels of the wicked nobility, parsimonious landowners, bogus scholars, untrustworthy geomancers, and ignorant schoolmasters; all in turn became objects of poetic attack, lashed by the malice of his words as his resentment and bitterness took on new forms.

Above the Governor's office swarm hordes of bandits.
Below the People's Pleasure Pavilion fall people's tears.
In Hamkyong Province all flee in shock;
Cho Ki-yong's family fortunes will not last long!

This satire against Cho Ki-yong, the Governor-General of Hamkyong Province, dexterously mixes various homonyms, using different Chinese characters in the two halves of each line. Characters with identical sounds can mean "the Governor's office" and "hordes of bandits", "The People's Pleasure Pavilion" and "people's tears", "Hamkyong Province" and "flee in shock", while the name of the Governor-General is the same as a term describing things that will not last long. The tone of the satire is remarkably severe.

A nobleman's brat with a wide high hat smokes a
 long-stemmed pipe
As he pretends to read a newly-bought book of Mencius's
 works;
He sounds like a monkey newly born by daylight
Or a frog roughly croaking in a twilight pond.

Geomancers are all fakes.
Tongues wagging, busily pointing out North and South.
If there's really a propitious site in those hills,
Why did you not bury your own father there?

These two poems mock the son of a rich nobleman and a geomancer, but they still observe the basic rules of poetry. Malice, however, expands easily and is difficult to contract, so that in his later poems as time went on such people become the objects of vicious ridicule. When certain Chinese words are spoken aloud they become the homophones of native Korean words; in this way the Chinese word for village school sounds like the Korean for "my prick", the scholar in his room is "a dog's dick", students become "mother-fuckers" and their teacher "my balls". In the same vein he makes a monk's head into "a horse's sweaty dick" and a scholar's topknot "the dangling dick of a squatting dog".

As changes occurred in the forms and themes, his expressive methods also changed. In place of rich and flowery rhetoric and a broad, leisurely development of emotions, wit and intelligence, novelty and originality become his main technical goals. The unconventional measures in the forms mentioned previously may have been provoked by the same pursuit.

As his poems changed, the class of his consumers also changed. The upper-class patrons of the last six or seven years turned their backs on him in anger or displeasure, and instead the lower-class multitude drew round him with their noisy applause. They might be deemed insignificant by the central government, they nevertheless appreciated his sharp satire and mockery of those who acted as their petty oppressors and exploiters; indeed, for a society as closed as that of the later Choson Dynasty, he sometimes played the role of a severe critic. Moreover, his relationship as Kim Ik-sun's grandson helped arouse a favourable inclination among the lower-class people of the Kwanso region. For as was seen earlier, deep in their hearts they still retained a feeling of compassion for Hong Kyong-rae and that feeling extended to him by way of his grandfather.

The intoxication resulting from the plaudits of the multitude was tremendous. Previously, his name had been unknown outside of the guest rooms of the landed gentry of Hamkyong Province; but now it spread in the space of a couple of years into every town and even the remote mountain villages of Pyongan Province. He no longer had to display his talents first before begging for food and shelter. As soon as they saw his bamboo hat, people welcomed him warmly into their houses and shared with him their vegetable gruel and weak rice wine. Yet there was no comparison between the intoxication those gave and the rich food or strong drink he had known previously.

The applause of the populace and his own sense of intoxication drove him even higher. In order to maintain the level of acclaim he was receiving, he set about intensifying his malice against society and increasing the unconventionality of his poems. Instead of the overall structure of a poem, he gave first priority to introducing novelties in the use of individual words and phrases. It was not so much that he was a frivolous man by nature, but the intoxication caused by the cheers of the multitude was too powerful. And they did not disappoint him. Whereas the learned and wealthy had pretended to know better and had been stingy in their praises, the ordinary people were generous in the expression of their emotions, while that acted on him as a new demand. Such was the process by which his poetry acquired its popular quality.

Some people question the authenticity of his popular identity, on the grounds that in his critiques there is no hint of any concern for structural matters, be it the monarchy as such, or the role of powerful families in politics, or the disorders in land administration, food supplies and military affairs; indeed, his satire and mockery were often directed against people who had themselves barely escaped becoming victims of the system, or those who were close to it. It is certainly true that among the poems of this period, there are many satirical works that may be suspected of being inspired by private feelings rather than by any objective critical consciousness.

However, an expression like "structural approach" may have a powerful appeal in a pretentious age like today, but not even the first pale shoots of it had begun to appear in his lifetime. Even for the most radically critical minds among the country's leading rich and powerful families, if something was wrong it was always seen as merely the fault of some individual, ranging from the benighted king at the top, right on down to the rapacious clerks in local magistrates' offices at the lowest level; they were incapable of harbouring any doubts about the monarchy as such, or the system of government by three premiers and six ministers. Naturally this only ended in his mocking and making fun of the petty malice or the follies of the class of people he met as he moved through the remote country villages; yet, as mentioned earlier, even that could prove effective as a serious form of social criticism.

It would be possible to criticize his ability and determination to act. If he really had a popular spirit, how was it he did nothing but sit tight with his back to the people and twist words around?

Even if he himself could not act, might he not have stirred up the people and incited them to resist? But perhaps even that is an absurd question, in view of the times he lived through and the spirit of the age. In a word, it was not yet an age of action, the time was not ripe for the people's sense of resistance to be set ablaze by an aesthetic critical spirit. It was more than half a century later that the Tonghak Movement rose like a giant maelstrom, but even then what provoked the people to action was no aesthetic critical spirit but a dark force in religious form.

If there is anything at all to be objected to in his popular spirit in that period, it would be that his popular qualities had led him to surrender too deeply to an undiscriminating populism. This is largely to be blamed on the times he lived in, but he was so unable to distinguish between popular spirit and popularity that together with the applause he accepted indiscriminately all kinds of pressing demands coming from the masses, without any filtering. As a result, although the themes of his poetry grew more varied, now including songs about passionate love and worldly affairs, in the end his poetry could not avoid losing its quality as it was fatally drawn towards popular taste by the force of that intense affinity.

> The man sucks up there,
> The girl down there.
> Up and down may differ,
> The taste is the same.

Quoting as his work such a poem, which seems to have been composed during this period, is enough to make one blush.

28

The world did not accept him like that for long, however. The poets of lower-class origin became jealous of his popularity and were the first to attack him. They did not spare him, exposing his every possible weakness, ranging from the liaisons with women, which started as soon as he established contact with lower-class people, to his excessively destructive approach to poetic form.

His sexual extravagance at this time was sufficiently immoderate to become the subject of gossip among later generations. Deeply hurt by the falsity and emptiness of the ink-smeared love found in the chambers of *kisaeng* girls, he turned to the dust-covered, sweaty-smelling women of the common class as if he was taking revenge on their whole sex. Perhaps it was really an unusual kind of ritual of affinity with the people at the very bottom of society that he was now eager to approach, rather than a pursuit of sexual pleasure as such. He felt as if he had truly become one with the simple common folk when he made love with one of them, with a forest tiller's daughter with a blooming, bright complexion despite a diet that included more grass-roots and tree-bark than corn, or with the wife of some peasant who lifted her hemp skirt for him while her husband was out for a few hours at the local market, their bodies locked like two guiltless wild beasts in a thicket or in a barley-field furrow.

> We met on the street; too many eyes watching!
> I like you, but I cannot speak; I may seem cold.
> It's not hard to climb the wall and make a hole,
> I'm already a farmer's, no help for it now.

This poem is written from the point of view of a peasant woman he could not possess, but readers in later generations have wondered whether the relationship really was left unfulfilled if there was such a degree of intimacy between them. During this period he mixed with all sorts of women, regardless of whether they were pretty or not, young or old, of noble or humble origin; but as soon as the world began to hate him, his love affairs became the object of severe criticism in tandem with his unconventional poetic practices.

Apart from such obvious forms of hostility, the criticisms raised by scholars of the traditional school were equally sharp. One Yo Kyu-hyong, a scholar who was referred to as a living "Anthology of Classical poetry" in the later period of the Choson Dynasty, wrote about his poetry in his own anthology of poems and essays, saying notably:

> The man called Kim the Bamboo Hat is such an eccentric, his visions are closed and uneven, like a rice jar tilted sideways. The elegance of his poetry is like that of someone who has just fallen into a thorn bush. He aims to be a poet, but his intentions are

> too vague for anyone to grasp his meaning, though it is hard to listen to him without feeling compassion. He is boisterous, he laughs readily and loses his temper easily; he is rough, yet he has the fault of being too soft.

Such comments seem to have been based on the impressions given by his poetry in its second phase.

Obviously there was a sense of resistance arising from the depths of himself. After five or six years of boisterous life he slowly began to sober up from the intense intoxication caused by popular acclaim, looking into himself and the state of his poetry in a kind of stupor.

He was so sure that he had become one with the weak and powerless at the lowest rung of society; he never doubted the sincerity of his love for them, even when he was not sure of what he believed. He proclaimed with great confidence that the malice he showed towards the rich and powerful was expressed on behalf of the lowest strata of society. When he engaged his talents in low-quality satire, with mockery verging on the obscene in its vituperation, he firmly announced that that was the only way for him to be faithful to their honest desires.

It was none of it true, though. As time passed, he came to realize that there remained in the inner recesses of his heart a conviction that he was doing them a great favour, even while he thought that he had become one of them, and he suffered intense anguish at the feeling that he was being hopelessly false. Even his affection for them was at best nothing more than a matter of bearing with their ignorance, their shallowness, selfishness and subservience; he had not positively embraced them, rolling in pain with them.

On close analysis, his belief that he had spoken on their behalf turned out to be only an excuse while he was in fact expressing his own personal grudge against society; a suspicion arose in his heart that even his claim to be obeying their desires was nothing more than flattery of poor-quality work. Towards the end of this period, he slowly developed a deep sense of shame at the thought that he too was a parasite, though in a different way, battening on the grudges of the foolish, helpless lowest classes, even an oppressor or exploiter on a limited scale.

He felt even more confused when he reviewed the mess he had made of his poetry. Undoubtedly, the common people's mode of life and forms of sensitivity possessed some of the typical attributes of the period's culture, yet their life and feelings as such could not be considered a culture.

Culture was something constituted through a filtering of the ordinary and the diverse, while poetry was an art that systematized those characteristics of culture in the severest manner. Yet using the ordinary people's simplicity as an excuse, claiming to be giving honest expression to their feelings, invoking their exuberance and their freedom, he had plunged his poetic art into a mire of diversity and plain-speaking, for which he felt utterly miserable.

All through this period, he was obliged to cling on to the emotion of hatred until in the end it turned into disgust and weariness. The characteristic features of the poems he wrote in these years, the satire, the mockery and jeering, were all essentially based on hatred and malice. In actual fact, his enmity toward the world was at its most intense during this period. Hatred and enmity are basically tensions that are bound to provoke weariness if they last too long. He was gradually becoming disgusted at having to express time after time the same hostility and antagonism.

I'm wasting my poetry like this! As he detached himself from the noisy crowds that had surrounded him before, and reflected alone on his poetry, he sometimes became apprehensive.

Besides, in the course of his years of travel through the Kwanso region, he finally gained more information about Hong Kyong-rae. An old man he encountered by chance one day gave him knowledge that undermined the very foundations of the second phase of his poetry on which he had embarked so triumphantly.

"In the end, you know," he was told, "Hong Kyong-rae and his gang were no different from the king and his ministers at the royal court, I mean all who regarded power and authority as the highest good and did not hesitate to do whatever was necessary in order to grasp them. A Righteous Cause? Of course, outwardly there was something like that. But if you look at it from another angle, you'll see that the goal they were really pursuing was to take the place of those who had gained control of all the privileges at court and excluded them. The poor folk who followed them? Don't make me laugh! Shall I tell you what their supporters were like, compared with those who now support the *status quo*? They were the alienated local gentry who harboured a grudge against the successful nobility of the capital; the newly rising landowners who quailed before the authority and cultural traditions of the existing land-owning class because of their humble origins and shallow education, even if they had managed to save money and buy some bits of land; the merchants of the Kaesong district whose commercial interests had been encroached on by the merchants from Seoul who enjoyed the support of the central government; mining speculators and wandering labourers whose life was relatively unstable compared with the peasants who relied on the land for their living, whether they had enough to eat or starved; there were members of the local militias, too, and clerks in magistrates' offices, all with grudges against the high officials appointed and sent by the central government. Those were the basis of Hong Kyong-rae's forces. If such people take responsibility for a righteous cause, while bearing obvious grudges against the existing privileged class, what do you expect? Being so divided, surely they would be prepared to say anything to bring even a single stupid commoner under their banner? Of course, some folk may have innocently believed them and decided to take up their cause, but those are only poor victims, and not a proof that Hong Kyong-rae was a righteous man. The widespread feelings among the low-class people in this area? You ought not to trust that. It's a particular emotion generated locally among the Kwanso population, a bitterness born when they saw their fathers, brothers and husbands being killed, innocent and guilty alike, by the government troops. Bitter feelings on their own are too weak and impotent, so they drew on the idea of a righteous cause that Hong Kyong-rae had invented to mobilize them. So don't go making a lot of noise about Hong Kyong-rae's righteousness, or about your grandfather; because he was unlucky enough to get caught up in those months' commotion he died shamefully in the eyes of both camps. I'm sure you bear resentment and bitterness inside yourself; but there was no great righteous cause capable of transcending society's systems and traditions."

That was what the white-haired old scholar quietly told him one autumn day, after he had been in the Kwanso region for nearly five years; it was during a visit he made to Myohyang Mountain, accompanied by people who had generously supplied him with food and drinks for several months while he was in Anju. The scholar belonged to the local gentry of Kwaksan and when young had at first taken part in the plotting of Hong Kyong-rae, Wu Kun-chik and Yi Hi-jo but soon, growing disillusioned with their so-called righteous cause and other such ideas, he had washed his hands of them and gone to live in hiding up in the mountains.

Starting with that, together with various points he had already felt doubtful about, slowly his new discoveries began to diminish the impact of the emotion provoked by Won Myong-dae five years before in Dabok Village. It became obvious that Won Myong-dae, only eighteen at the time and with a simple soldierly character, had exaggerated, making the righteous cause of Hong Kyong-rae much larger and more splendid than it had actually been in his account of it. The same was true of his interpretation of his grandfather. Won Myong-dae had seen what he wanted to see and had understood his grandfather as he wanted to understand him.

Eventually, his feelings of resentment and bitterness were forced to return to what they had been before. Indeed, all his emotions were forced back to their previous state. In the end, his poetry too. But he had gone too far. His reputation in the eyes of the world had for long now been on a road of no return; likewise his poetry. During this period he frequently dreamed he had fallen into a swamp, from which he was struggling desperately to escape, but to no avail.

29

It was not long, however, before he had an opportunity to escape from that helpless state in which his poetry was mired, although it was an enormously cruel experience for him. It was the spring of his thirty-eighth year.

Savage lands have no flowers.
Savage lands have no flowers?
Savage lands have no flowers, they say.
But how can a land have no flowers?

He had spent the whole winter in the market town of Kaechon. On that day, as on any other, he had managed to impress various groups of people at the market with a bogus poem in the morning, and got them to buy him drinks. Yet all the while he felt depressed, and was sitting in an inn alone when someone came looking for him.

"A scholar called Noh Jin asked me to deliver this poem to you with his best wishes for your health. He would like to hear what comments a renowned poet like yourself has to make about it. He asks you to read it."

A man in servant's dress had asked the innkeeper where the poet was, and had presented him with a letter. At the name of Noh Jin, he felt his heart sink, and when he opened the envelope, instead of a letter he drew out a familiar-looking piece of poetry. He quickly read it through:

Kim Ik-sun, you were a great loyal subject
  descended from generations,
while Chong was nothing but a mediocre official.
Your family was that of the mighty Kims,
  the clan of the Changdong Kims,
Your given name of Sun was renowned throughout the
  capital.
Yet you gained the reputation of one
  who surrendered to barbarians
and Chong earned a hero's name equal to that of Yue Fei.

There were only six lines out of the original thirty-six, but it was clearly the poem he had composed at the poetry competition in Chongson nineteen years before. That poem he longed to forget, yet could not forget. Noh Jin too he longed to forget, like the poem, yet could not. "But why has he sent me this poem?" he wondered, while he rubbed his chest with one hand, as the former pain seemed suddenly to revive. But the pain only grew more acute, while he still could not fathom what was Noh Jin's intention.

"Well, sir? The master told me to bring back your reply."

The man in servant's clothes asked him this while he felt vacant. He thought he saw a faint mocking smile on the man's lips. As if prompted by that, he seemed to hear Noh Jin's cold voice ringing in his ear.

"Once you were busy getting social promotion by selling your grandfather's name. Now you are enjoying a false reputation in the market streets by using the same grandfather's name. Aren't you sneaking a ride on the common people's resentment, and making a living out of it for yourself? You shameless wretch, do you dare say you write poetry?"

If his belief in Hong Kyong-rae and in his grandfather had not been shaken to the very roots by this time, that voice might not have shocked him so much. He pressed both hands to his breast, feeling a pain more intense than that of nineteen years ago. Once more the servant asked him:

"What do you think, sir? What reply shall I take back?"

"It's very well written . . ."

He had scarcely said it, when he felt a nauseous lump rise suddenly into his throat. Taken by surprise, he spat it out and saw it was a clot of crimson blood, just like nineteen years before.

It is sometimes said that Noh Jin sent him that piece of poetry out of jealousy at his talent. That Noh Jin wrote that poem himself in an attempt to drive him out of the Kwanso region where Noh Jin claimed to be the best master in the rhetorical style of the government service examinations. It is wrong to attribute the authorship of that poem to Noh Jin, and above all it is going much too far to interpret Noh Jin's intention in so mundane a manner.

Nonetheless, after that incident he left Kwanso and never once set foot there again.

30

He felt deeply apprehensive as he left the Kwanso area; perhaps he might never again be able to write a poem? "I have lost poetry."

Having decided to believe that, he spent the next two years in a kind of frenzy of jesting and eccentric behaviour.

Yet he was still a poet for all that. Although it might undergo various transformations, poetry had become an essential way of living for him. Once the shock he had received back there in Kwanso had subsided and he had reached the less troubled age of forty, gradually his poetic inspiration began to spring up again, in a manner appropriate to his age. In spite of his apprehensions, his poetry entered a third phase of transformation.

The poetry of this period developed around a meditative, introspective feeling. Now, instead of the exaggerated emotionalism of the early period or the anti-social acrimony of the second phase, a warm sympathy and comprehension towards the whole of human life became the dominant emotion. Forms and techniques also changed. The passion for unconventional modes of writing found in the second period gave way to a respect for traditional norms, while the earlier attachment to techniques full of novelty and wit was gone.

> In a lonely tavern under a cold pine tree
> I recline at my leisure, like a man from a different world.
> I play with the clouds in valleys nearby,
> Enjoy bird-song for company beside the streams.
> Why should I grow rough because society is in uproar?
> I regale myself with poems and wine.
> When the moon rises, I recall old times
> And gently fall into sweet dreams.

This poem, entitled "Reciting for Myself", shows well the main characteristics of his poetry in this phase, while the next example, "A Bowl of Gruel", is equally representative of the period. This poem is widely read even today; it goes roughly as follows:

> The gruel in the bowl on this little four-legged table
> Is so thin it reflects the pale azure clouds.
> Please don't be ashamed, master of the house.
> Why, I love to see green hills reflected in water.

"On Seeing the Corpse of a Beggar" is likewise a poem from this same period, in which he reveals controlled emotions as he expresses his sympathy for an abandoned life:

> I don't know your first name, or your last.
> Which river, what mountain did you call home?
> Flies swarm in early sunlight to eat your rotten flesh,
> At sunset crows croak to comfort your lonely soul.
> One short walking-staff is all you bequeath,
> With two handfuls of rice you got by begging.
> I beg of you, villagers living just down the road,
> Bring one basket of earth to keep off the wind and frost.

In this period he showed his commiseration toward the poor and wretched, not only in poems but also in action. In the *Haejang Anthology* mentioned earlier can be found the following lines:

> In cold weather and hot, he always went about in thinly lined white clothes; once somebody made a new set of clothes for him, padded with cotton, which he put on without any fuss. He rolled up the clothes he had been wearing into a bundle that he slung over one shoulder and went on his way; along the road he met a man shivering with cold so he took off the padded clothes he was wearing and gave them to the man, donning once more the old clothes he had tied into a bundle . . .

He seems at this time to have been meditating on humanity and human existence, not from any superficial social consciousness, but viewing humanity as one part of Nature. Undoubtedly that was the way in which he found himself expressing the deeply-felt compassion inspired by mankind's inborn finiteness and solitude, the inescapable burden of weariness and sorrow.

It is not so very difficult to see why his poetry and his life underwent such a change. It is, however, a wearisome task and makes a boring tale, to keep trying to fathom the depths of some unknown person's consciousness and present that in a neat logical order. In short, it can be surmised that the aesthetic experience accumulated in the course of those two different phases in which he wrote two entirely different kinds of poetry, as well as a change in his aesthetic ideas due to age as he advanced into the latter part of his life, and the expanding depth of insight into the world he had gained, all combined to form the basis for that transformation.

Those old commonplaces about human existence that say "Man comes from Nature and goes back to it", or "Each one comes here alone and returns alone" ought to be enough to constitute one major factor in the maturation of a poet so plunged in meditation and introspection.

31

He went on his way. Walking along quiet hillside paths, with no sign of any other human being, his steps were light and quick. It was as if he was borne by the breeze when a breeze was blowing, floated after the clouds when clouds were floating, sought for wild flowers when he saw wild flowers, was lured by the birds when they were singing.

He had wasted a large part of his life in a journey through two diametrically opposed worlds and ways of knowing. First he had been obliged to pass through a world of affirmations, acceptances and conservatism, with its own ways of knowledge, devoting to that his childhood, beautiful though it might now seem with its loneliness and sorrows, to say nothing of a major part of his fiery youth. Life in that world assumed as its essential forms endurance, survival, achievement, and pleasure, while the main focus of knowledge was the conviction that whatever is happening *now* is utterly right, that whatever exists *here* must all necessarily be respected and preserved.

However, the star of deviation that was guiding his life did not allow him to stay and live content in such a world and way of knowing. As his youth was fading away in sorrow, a new world and way of knowing caught hold of his soul where it lay bleeding from the twists of a cruel fate. It demanded recognition that a world where living beings are forced to accept oppression, deprivation and agony, and all that is happening *now*, is utterly false and wrong, that whatever exists *here* must all necessarily be destroyed, then be born again.

He threw himself into that world and way of knowledge with a passion that was the more intense for being so dark. It too, however, was not a world in which one can grow old comfortably, not a way of knowledge allowing one to die in faith. Where can you find sunlight without shadows, outside without inside, front without back? Worlds and ways of knowing likewise had their double natures, the tensions between which were nothing but idle songs sung *here* and *now*.

After this, for a long while he spent dreary-seeming hours disputing as to which of the two was right or wrong. Sometimes he would rebuke the two antipodal worlds and ways of knowing together, as if he had come to a total understanding of the cosmos and life, and sometimes he would embrace them both, then writhe in agony. But since he had no final answer, he remained desolate; the two worlds and ways of knowing had turned their backs on him so stubbornly that he was left forlorn. The pursuit of moderation and harmony between those two, so radically opposed to one another, was not the end of disputes but their beginning. When the negatives dominated, inevitably the two became utter foes, while they did not become friends when the positives had the upper hand.

In the end, he turned with new expectation to Nature. He realized that his sense of desolation derived from his involvement in human disputes, and he therefore moved away from the villages and marketplaces, freeing himself from the consciousness of people who always felt unbearably empty and insecure if they had not opted for one side or another. His withdrawal was equally for the sake of his poetry, that was by now reeling from the wounds it had received from worldly disputes.

Ancient wisdom frequently derives from an intimation that Nature is the archetype of all knowledge, all beauty, all truth, all holiness. In actual fact, he too had nurtured his knowledge in accordance with such ancient wisdom, distinguishing the beautiful, the true, and the holy from all that was not so, and he strove to bring the imitation of that into his poems from the very start. But at that time he had not yet attained the contemplation, if we may call it that, the self-immersion that constitute the essence of the ancient roadway leading into Nature.

Now, however, it was different. Now he was exploring and searching the very depths of Nature; not the paradigm of Nature that forms the compulsory object of repetitious study, but Nature as the ideal model of all values, corresponding to the fundamental needs of the inner self. Although that unity or oneness with Nature that he and his poems strove so hard to attain, and perhaps in the end attained, was still far away, he was now entering a world and way of knowing quite different from his previous experience, in the sense that he was slowly moving away from considerations of utilitarian effectiveness.

Autumn was already far advanced and the mountainsides were covered with red maples so bright that the trees seemed ablaze. As he gazed at the sky, so blue it seemed the colour would come off if he passed a hand across it, and the contrasting brilliant red maple leaves, he realized that he recognized the spot. It was the slope at the foot of Ninth Moon Mountain that he had climbed one day in his remote childhood together with his father and elder brother, both of them now dead.

He did not know what so attracted him, but after the Diamond Mountains it was the mountain he visited most frequently. Though the road might vary, he passed that way almost every year, and this year, quite accidentally, he happened to pass by way of that lower slope which had remained so long buried in his childhood memories.

He was filled with sadness to realize that, while the mountain remained the same, he himself had changed: from being a boy of seven he was now a middle-aged man with hair already turning grey at the temples. One of the qualities people afterwards most admired about him was the way his sense of wit and humour transformed pathos and suffering into a fine poem in a moment. On that day, too, he tried to relieve the sadness that suddenly overwhelmed him by writing a comic poem:

Last year I passed by Ninth Moon Mountain at the ninth moon,
This year I passed by Ninth Moon Mountain at the ninth moon.
Every year I pass by Ninth Moon Mountain at the ninth moon,
Ninth Moon Mountain's beauty is always at the ninth moon.

While he was cooling himself under a maple tree, reciting to himself this seven-character quatrain with its eight repetitions of the same words, someone suddenly shouted in a harsh voice from the dark woods:

"Hey you! Don't move! If you do I'll bore a hole in your skull!"

He came to himself with a start and looked in the direction the voice had come from; a group of brigands was slowly advancing towards him, brandishing sabres and spears, while in their centre was a sturdy young man aiming a matchlock at him. There was nothing particularly surprising about it, bands of robbers could frequently be met with along the secluded hilltop paths.

In his time, robbers teemed in every deep mountain valley. Often all designated collectively as the Fire Brigands: there were the Bright Flame Brigands, the Vast Fire Party, the Green Forest Party, while on a somewhat larger scale there were gangs claiming to be the heirs of ancient bands such as the Poor Folks' Party and the Master-murdering Club.

They were for the most part vagrants, people who had fallen victim to the calamities such as drought, pestilence, or the conflicts between political factions, that marked the later Choson Era. But on closer scrutiny, they fell into two broad categories. One group had goods and property as their sole aim, any other claims they made were meant only to justify their having become robbers; the other group was composed of master brigands, different from the first in both aims and claims. There were not many of them, but some among those master brigands were determined to take over the world, proclaiming equality and prosperity for all.

It was not so very unusual for him to meet this kind of group in the long course of his wandering life. And he had few reasons to fear encounters with them, no matter who they were. Not only after he had begun to be widely known, but even before that, when he was still completely unknown, he was essentially the same kind of vagrant as they were and therefore was allowed to go free.

However, that day it was different. The group that had captured him showed no sign of recognition, though he produced his bamboo hat and cane and stated his identity as a poet; even after he told them that he was really just a poor underprivileged fellow like them, they refused to let him go. They coaxed him along, shouted him down, and finally led him off to their mountain lair.

It was only when he arrived in their fortress, situated in a secluded valley of Obong Mountain, that he realized he had fallen in with one of those bands of master brigands he had hitherto only heard about. Their lair was a stone-walled fortification, set in a precipitous spot at the far end of a valley, easy to defend but difficult to attack; it was quite unlike the dens of the petty thieves who robbed travellers of their bags along the road. The positioning of the guards and the discipline they observed were more rigorous than that found in any military camp.

Above all, what struck him most forcefully was their leader. In that middle-aged man with his swarthy and yet somehow pale face he could find none of the bravado and swagger often seen in such leaders. He had no seat covered with animal skins, but was sitting on a rush mat in a simple mud hut without any escorting bodyguards; after listening to a noisy report he emerged quietly into the courtyard. With his small stature he did not look particularly strong. What was astonishing was the attitude of respect his followers manifested. As soon as he emerged, all those men, numbering more than a hundred and ferocious as tigers, froze to the spot and respectfully brought their hands together in greeting.

The man scrutinized him silently, with no trace of expression on his face. The intense gaze seemed to come piercing through his cheeks and for some unknown reason it quite overwhelmed him. However, there was a faint hint of learning in his look and behaviour, which reassured him a little.

"I am merely a traveller with no possessions, captain. The only thing I have that you could take is my life, and it would be useless to you, so I hope you'll let me go."

When he spoke, feeling really frightened, the men nearby shot fierce warning glares at him.

"Don't call him captain, he's Master Chesei. If you take us for ordinary bandits and insult him, there'll be no mercy for you."

The men shouted at the top of their voices, yet not a sound seemed to reach the ears of the chieftain they called Master Chesei. He simply observed his prisoner for a while without a word, then spoke, quietly shaking his head.

"When our young comrades go out on long journeys and keep watch along the roads, it is not simply to get money. Sometimes they go out to take lives."

The voice was low but it had the effect of a cold wind blowing at his back.

"What do you hope to do with the lives you take?"

"It is not that we have any use for them; it is simply to reduce the number of useless lives that are wasting the world's resources."

"What kind of life do you consider to be useless?"

"Those who eat without working; those who expend without producing. I will ask you a question. Do you go out to work in the fields? Do you harvest for yourself the food you eat?"

At that, he felt he could guess what kind of a man this chieftain was. Here he was meeting by chance a mind placed at one extreme point of the conflicts he himself had experienced long before, standing here deep in the mountains exactly as if he was in some marketplace. He looked at him suddenly with a rising curiosity. The stillness of the man's features was like that found in deep waters, it reflected coldly an ideological conviction built up over a long period of time. For some reason it provoked his pride and made him speak frankly.

"No. I have not worked or harvested for many years now."

"Then have you woven cloth? Have you made others warm with that cloth and so earned food to eat?"

"No, not at all. And not only I, for no man in this country ever weaves cloth."

"Just answer my questions. Are you a craftsman, then? Can you forge or make tools that serve the common good?"

"No, not at all. I have never even sat near a bellows."

"Judging by your bundle, you seem not to be a trader who goes around distributing goods and living on the profits; judging by your face, you can't be a butcher. Then you must be a gentleman-scholar."

"No, not that either. I have never dreamed of becoming a statesman living on his annuity, have never wanted to become a scholar earning a living by his learning, I cannot be called a gentleman-scholar."

At that point in his replies, the chieftain's voice became cold and fierce.

"In any case, you are someone who eats without working and expends without producing. The lives we take belong to thieves like you."

Having anticipated from the start what might be coming, he was not unduly surprised, even at what might turn out to be a rigorous death sentence. He felt as if he was throwing a joke at a half-baked nobleman as he asked:

"I would like to ask you a question if I may, not at all with the thought of grovelling for my life, but to satisfy my curiosity: could you please tell me what you yourself produce? What do you produce in order to get what you need to eat, to dress, to expend?"

"I have produced dreams for the poor to believe in and rely on, I have produced future days they can wait for patiently. And in future I want to produce a better world."

"Well then, I also produce. I have produced poetry."

"You say you have produced poetry?"

"I would never suggest to a person like you that poetry as such is something produced. But if dreams can be said to be produced, and hopes, then perhaps poetry too can be termed a production. For poetry too can produce dreams and hopes. But surely, if you want to produce a better world, you will need far more than you say? Other emotions, besides dreams and hopes. Now poetry can be a useful tool in producing those other emotions."

He had not been mistaken in guessing that the man had a background of brush and ink. There was no way of telling what stage he had reached in the course of his studies before the direction of his life had changed, but at least he knew the outward value of poetry. The man studied him again for a while in silence, then asked:

"Without doubt, to produce a better world, many more things are necessary. Tell me, now. Can you, by means of poetry, produce fear and a feeling of impotence?"

"It is possible."

"And can you likewise produce courage and belief?"

"That too is possible."

"In that case, you are someone who produces. You may live and continue to dress, eat and expend. But you must stay here and produce for us. You must labour to produce fear and impotence in our enemies, courage and belief in our comrades here and those who are on our side down below."

Naturally he understood what the man wanted. This master brigand was asking for his help in the production of his ultimate goal by employing one of the functions of poetry that he had rejected, considering it too worldly a role, although some people simply called it utilitarian.

Yet, without quite knowing why, he felt a sudden temptation. No doubt it was because he had never been able to explore thoroughly such roles, occupied as he had been in throwing the market streets into turmoil with his noisy effusions as a "people's poet". In those days the most his poetry had done was to poke fun at the rich and powerful, but that only made them look ridiculous so that people laughed, it could never make them shake with fear; it merely expressed sympathy and compassion for the poor and weak, it could never make them all rise up together to open the way to a new world by the courage and belief it gave them.

"Perhaps so far I have only been peeling away the husk of the world and ways of knowing? I have devoted myself passionately to denial and rejection, but it seems that the essential core of the world and its knowledge does not lie there but rather in the will to destroy and create anew, tasks that I have neglected. To break down the old, corrupt world and open the way for a new, more liveable world! Why, if ever my poetry could help to achieve even one little part of that task, it would be performing a great service! Who knows, perhaps that great service may take the place of whatever that undefinable thing is that I am at present trying to find in Nature."

He went so far as to entertain such belated expectations. But before he undertook to produce what this master brigand wanted, there was one question bothering him that he needed an answer to:

"What do you think about producing voluntary remorse? What about the will to change oneself beginning from the top? Don't you think that if you produced such things and distributed them among your enemies, you might be able to open the way to a better world without harsh, violent battle?"

He asked the question cautiously. Master Chesei's expression changed for the first time.

"Such things must not be produced! It's not just that it is very difficult to produce them; it has already been clearly established in the course of thousands of years of history that they serve no purpose even if they are produced. When did the rich and powerful ever repent and change voluntarily? If the world had been changing, even ever so slowly, over the thousands and thousands of years since it began, would it be in the shape it's in now? They merely pretend to change if they find they cannot keep on any longer as they are. What difference does it make to a hungry monkey if you vary the rules and give it four acorns in the morning and three in the evening instead of three in the morning and four in the evening?"

"That is not quite so. For example, the productions of Confucius and Mencius have undoubtedly changed the substance of the world for the better. Certainly they taught the poor and underprivileged to bow their heads and accept their lot patiently, but didn't they also advise the powerful and wealthy to examine their consciences and amend their lives? And in the times when their productions were respected, did the world not clearly become a better place than it had been before?"

"That is precisely the reason why I hate those long-bearded scholars with their high hats. They have been extolling Confucius and Mencius for two thousand years now, but how much has the world changed for the better in all that time? Those scholarly curs have simply used the produce of Confucius and Mencius as a way of currying favour with the high and mighty! While they are out among the common people they talk of the demands of the royal way and discuss the humanity and justice required of those who rule; once they get into royal service, all they do, every man jack of them, is bark at their master's command."

His voice, that had so far only been vehement, now became a cutting sword.

"We cannot wait any longer. It would be more harmful for us to say that the rich and powerful can show remorse and reform themselves voluntarily and that therefore the world can become a better place without a revolution, than to believe that the world as it is is good enough. How long have we been waiting? Are you saying that we ought to wait still longer, deluded by that kind of hopeless talk?"

There may be various explanations as to why he stayed without the least resistance up in the mountain fortress and devoted himself for a while to that strange form of production. One reason could be his reluctance to throw away his life for nothing; another might be a newly-aroused interest in the world of those living at the foot of the mountain, motivated by the fresh shock he had received from the Master's logic. But probably the most important thing of all was his curiosity as a poet.

In actual fact, the ideas on the place of poetry and its uses which this man propounded as a creed were neither very unfamiliar nor very new to him. Yet this opportunity to apply poetic theory to a concrete situation and confirm its truthfulness by direct observation, was bound to exercise a fascination that no poet could easily forgo. Whatever the reason, he stayed in the mountain fortress and readily put his poetic skills at their service.

32

Soon winter came and the mountain stronghold was buried deep in snow. Because it was hard to go down from the fortress in a big group in the snow, and because there was nothing to be gained by lurking along the paths since they were blocked, the entire band spent the winter holed up in the camp, with the exception of a few nimble-footed youths who went to spy secretly in the nearby villages and some who kept watch at the top of the mountain behind the fortress.

The vision that Master Chesei produced and distributed among them all was far more wide-ranging and detailed than might at first appear. Old ideals and systems, including republican notions of universal harmony, the Taedong system of tax reform, the Chongjon proposal on land reform, the Kyunsu system for an equal distribution of goods, and others, were all delicately woven together to form the basis of his dream of the better world he hoped to produce, and indeed, if it had only been possible to accomplish it, nothing could have been better. Besides, at first sight the methods and processes for the production of the dream were organized in a practical and coherent manner. First they had to prepare water where the fish could swim, then get the fish to multiply in number; finally they would take to the dry land and sweep everything before them; they were already well advanced with the first stage. While keeping Ninth Moon Mountain as their main base, their plan was to launch attacks on the nearby townships and so, by increasing the area not under government control, to increase as much as possible the area of water where they could swim.

The place that Master Chesei had in mind as the first area to be removed from government control was the town of Sinchon. Once spring came the plan was to force their way into the administrative offices there and gain control of the official seal; then they would hold out as long as they could, meanwhile so overawing the whole township that in future it would remain water they could swim in. For even if government troops arrived in force and retook the town, driving them back into their mountain fastness, the citizens would find it hard to ignore a power that had once controlled their lives.

While Master Chesei and his young comrades were undergoing hard mental and physical training in preparation for the coming spring, he devoted himself to the production he had promised them. At least, with the themes fixed in advance and the purpose clear, that kind of production was bound to prove easier than any he had previously tried. For the only thing he had to work hard on boiled down to a question of technical challenges involving the right choice of words and the adjustment of rhythm and rhyme.

Before very long he began to pour out his produce and Master Chesei chose those poems which he thought would help his own production most effectively, distributing them according to the plans he had made. As midwinter drew near, the comrades in the fortress started using new songs to heighten their hostility, nourishing their courage and belief. Most of the works he produced at this time are lost, but a few have been handed down:

> On Ninth Moon Mountain snow is falling.
> Raise swords and spears, we're off to war.
> Comrades killed, felled by the foes' swords
> I'll repay your enemies now.
>
> Raise aloft our righteous banner
> Under it we'll fight and die.
> Cowards, go, if you want to.
> We'll defend the banner here.
>
> Don't lament us when we're dead.
> We gave our lives fighting the foe.
> Each drop of blood we shed will blossom,
> Flowering as a better world.

Another batch of songs which he produced was delivered by the young comrades who went to reconnoitre in the villages at the foot of the mountain for the benefit of their enemies there. Not songs for their enemies to sing, of course, but to hear being sung.

Soon after the lunar New Year, eerie songs unlike any ever heard before began to spread in the town of Sinchon. A young serf chopping fodder for the cows could be heard humming to himself:

> In the dark, a lamp hung up, I chop the hay.
> My limbs are weary from the weight of firewood on my back.
> Slicing away, slicing away, I chop the hay.

I'll chop off the white hands of the rich
And cut off greedy officials' heads too.

A butcher sitting astride a writhing pig could be heard singing enthusiastically as he cut its throat:

Today I'm killing a pig for you
To make your belly fatter still.
I cut the pig's throat with a hungry stomach,
One day my knife will cut your throat,
I'll slice out that thick fat paunch of yours.

And the wife of an old peasant would suddenly start singing a weeding-song in the midst of her night-long weaving:

Hey now, comrades all, let's go to the fields and weed.
Foxtail, cocklebur, sedges, and worts,
Let's root them out and burn them up.
So much for the fields, but who'll weed the world?

The scholars and the rich, who will get rid of them?
Let's not worry! Ninth Moon Mountain's there!
Ninth Moon Mountain comrades will weed the world.
They'll make a better world, no scholars, no rich men.

As Master Chesei had anticipated, these products proved highly effective. The young comrades up in the fortress, eager to set about making a new world, deplored the spring's slowness in coming; some even came to the Master and urged him to attack in the snow. They were all so full of burning hatred for the enemy, of death-defying courage, and an invincible belief in victory, that they could no longer be satisfied with only killing in songs, dying in songs, and winning victories in songs.

The effect in the villages at the foot of the mountain was equally remarkable. Though the songs were only sung in secret among the lower classes, some members of the upper class inevitably had sharp ears and before the first month of the year was out, the songs were known among the nobles and the rich merchants in Sinchon and even by the officials in the local government office. Shocked by their extraordinary, cruel contents, the magistrate sent out emissaries to investigate the matter and, at the same time, tried to forbid the songs, but to no avail. The harder they tried to suppress the songs, the faster they spread, bringing in their wake a wave of fear and helplessness that spread like an epidemic. Some of the rich and noble families panicked, packed up their belongings and moved into nearby cities with high and solid fortifications, or went all the way to the capital to be close to the king and the metropolitan garrison.

Thanks to the effectiveness of his productions, the author of the songs was treated like a staff officer or a high-ranking official. Even the Master, who had for a time acted towards him in a cold, stern manner, warmed and finally accepted him as a real companion. Yet none of that made him feel happy or cheerful. All he experienced that winter was a sense of anxiety and impatience, not unlike what a scholar feels when he has left an examination after handing in an unsatisfactory paper.

At long last the apparently interminable winter ended and spring came. As the snow that had been piled deep on all sides of the mountain melted, the roads below opened to traffic and news began to arrive from faraway places that had been cut off. Once they had entered the second month of the year, occasional passers-by brought news of insurrections that had troubled the southern regions, while an epidemic had ravaged Kwanbuk, leaving the population restless and rebellious.

As soon as the roads leading down from the mountain were open, the young comrades began to manifest an agitation that Master Chesei was only able to restrain with difficulty; therefore once these reports were confirmed he decided to launch the attack at once. He had originally intended to wait for the spring famine before moving, when there might be more widespread disturbances, but he judged from the rumours coming in that the time was already ripe.

The day of battle the young comrades in the fortress had been awaiting for so long dawned at last. On the third day of the third month almost two hundred of them, armed with the weapons they had spent the winter forging and sharpening, to say nothing of the courage and faith resulting from their prolonged training as well as from the songs produced for them, headed down towards Sinchon, which they had targeted from the first. Their spirits were high, not only because several times they had attacked the place and taken bounty, but because this time they were better prepared than ever before.

"You may not be able to carry weapons and fight, still, you must go down with us. You need to check for yourself the result of your products so as to prepare an even more effective production in times to come."

At Master Chesei's command he joined the rearguard ranks of their company. Killing and destruction were not for him, but the uneasiness he felt made him eager to verify the result of what he had produced. Perhaps too, unconsciously, he was hoping he might find an opportunity of breaking free from the abstractions of Nature and return to the more definite world of disputes and conflicts found in populated streets and villages.

They left the fortress at noon and arrived at dawn the next morning in the hills behind Sinchon; there they spent the day resting. After they had recovered from the fatigue caused by the all-night march, they planned to wait for nightfall then launch a surprise attack on the government offices.

Things began to go wrong from that point onward. On previous expeditions they had remained hidden in the bushes in a deathly silence and waited for night to fall, but that day was different. Under the combined influence of Master and poet, they threw to the winds all the caution that they naturally should have observed. On account of the groundless emotions filling them, the product of mere ideals unrelated to their real strength, the valley where they were hiding rang with unnecessary noise; detected by woodcutters and the village women coming to gather early spring shoots, they had already been reported to the local government office before sunset. They made a grave error by not marching straight to their target that morning, weary though they were.

The poems he produced and sent down to the enemy had failed to instil the degree of fear and helplessness that Master Chesei had counted on. Many of the town's rich people, government officials and their clerks, had been seized with fear at the hair-raising songs that had appeared as if from nowhere during the winter months, as well as the strange atmosphere reigning among the lower classes. That in turn inevitably developed into a sense of powerlessness and defeatism, given the corruption of the central government from which they could expect little help. Such people had moved away to the capital or to larger fortresses where there was a commander in charge of the defence.

It was quite another matter for those who felt they had too much to lose to be able to leave their lands, or those who for one reason or another were obliged to share the fate of the system as a whole. Their defensive instincts were aroused and, fired not by mere emotions but by a resolute will to survive, they prepared to repel the attack of this gang of unusual thieves. They brought out and cleaned rusty weapons that had for long been lying neglected, and repaired the crumbling fortifications. They cajoled disgruntled military officers into taking up their swords, gave food to those who were starving by reason of the prolonged winter, and so to some degree calmed the anxieties of the citizens. Being warned in advance of the brigands' movements thanks to the negligence with which they approached the town, they were able to set up a truly cast-iron defence.

It was the second watch, around ten in the evening, when the bandits came down, fending the darkness only to find the local government office lit up by torches as bright as broad daylight and surrounded by a force numbering several hundreds composed of regular soldiers and local reservists reinforced by a large number of youths. Unable to grasp this unexpected turn of events, Master Chesei exclaimed:

"What in the world is happening?"

He too was at first unable to take it in. A poet he might be, yet how could even he be expected to grasp the subtle laws by which, no matter how corrupt an existing system may be, there will always be people who have no choice but to defend it, while fear can inspire such people with a truly desperate courage and determination? Yet even now, Master Chesei interpreted the situation in their favour.

"They're at their wits' end! Don't be taken in by their bluff!"

At Master Chesei's order the band of young comrades, still intoxicated by their songs, enthusiastically launched their doomed assault. Shouting battle cries, they aimed their matchlocks, waved spears and swords as they advanced, but the final outcome was a disaster. Even before they reached the wall of the government office, a dozen or so of the comrades had been hit by arrows and then, on reaching the wall, another half-dozen fell like straws before the defenders' swords.

In the end, what made their defeat all the more decisive was the qualitative change that had occurred within them. In the days when they had had no view of the future, no fantasies about a better world, they had been brave men. So long as they were nothing but ignorant bandits full of desperate violence and undefined resentment, they were ready to go through fire and water in battle; but now they had become completely different men, after a whole winter's baptism into Master Chesei's reasoning and their poet's emotionalism. Having begun to use their reason, they started to reason about their own lives; and as they began to control emotions with the poems their poet had produced, to some degree art had weakened them. All winter long they had been slaughtering hosts of rich people and corrupt officials in words, procuring for themselves a vicarious satisfaction that now proved a hindrance in obtaining from them the courage they had formerly displayed.

"My young comrades, what has happened to you? What has become of your former courage and fighting spirit?"

Coming across one group running away in disarray in the midst of the battle, Master Chesei could not hide his dismay.

"The enemy's too strong! We need to go back to the fortress and make ourselves stronger so we can beat them."

The young fellows used reasoning in their reply. Their eyes were showing obvious signs of fear but they stubbornly tried to deny the fact.

"If you order us all to charge in and die, we'll do it. But in that case, who will open the way to the new world? Who will save the poor mired in their misery?"

In the meanwhile a large group of townsfolk had gathered near the government office. The Master suddenly shifted his attention to them, as he cried out:

"What are you all doing? Help us drive out corrupt officials and their rotten regime, let's build a new world! Let's make a nation where you will be in charge!"

Their reaction, too, was completely different from what he expected. These were people who had previously sided with them in secret even if they could not help openly. Now that the products of Master and poet had combined, they naturally ought to have been rushing forward with open arms but it was not happening. They too had been fed full of emotions and reasoning. All winter long they had been cutting the throats and slitting the bellies of countless hated scholars and officials in song; after that they felt if anything less inclined than ever to rise up with real swords in their hands. Instead, they had developed a spectator psychology and they just stood there, gaping at a distance, as they waited to see what the next bit of fun might be.

Master Chesei nearly forced the young comrades from the spot and charged the office once more, but without the support of the townspeople they were too few in number. Again they lost a dozen or so men and were driven back a couple of miles by the soldiers, who had now regained their self-confidence, before they were able to regroup.

"There's nothing more to be done now. Let's ransack some isolated rich houses then go back up to the fort. Once we're there we'll recharge our strength and plan for the future."

Master Chesei changed their goal. But that too did not work out as planned. Not a single bag of rice nor a yard of silk remained in the houses of those rich families who had taken fright and fled to the larger towns, while those who were too fat to move had made their own preparations against attack. They had given dozens of sturdy young farm hands plenty of food to eat then set them up as guards, at the same time creating lines of communication with the neighbouring farmers, so that when they attacked such a house they found it was as well defended as the government office had been.

On top of which each household had several fast horses ready to send for help to nearby rich houses and the government office, so there was absolutely nothing they could do.

After their first attack on a wealthy house had ended in failure, as they were moving on to another Master Chesei asked with a sigh:

"How is it that even this kind of people have decided to stay put and fight?"

"Perhaps because they have nowhere to run away to? Our songs have made them realize that . . ."

He spoke bitterly but left the sentence unfinished.

The second house they attacked was smaller in size than the first and the number of guards was less. There too a horse had been sent out to fetch help, but judging by the number of arrows being shot from inside and the brightness of the torchlight, the band of young comrades might have been able to rob it and leave again before the troops arrived, if they had only tried a little harder.

Perhaps because they had already been obliged to take to their heels twice, here they failed even to scale the flimsy outer wall of the house. They made a lot of noise, shouting to one another in loud voices, but even when they finally moved to attack, it only took a few arrows flying out to send them retreating helter-skelter.

News must have got through, and the red glow of the torches borne by the soldiers coming to the rescue could be seen drawing near.

"It's too late! Retreat!"

At last Master Chesei gave up, shouting the order in agonized tones.

By the time they shook off their pursuers and arrived back at the foot of the mountain where the way led up to their fastness, day was already breaking. Master Chesei took his seat on a broad flat rock, first ordering his men to go and rest on a secluded, sheltered ridge; some were wounded, all were deadly tired from the futile all-night battle. Then he shut both eyes, and seemed plunged deep in thought. Drawn somehow by an uneasy feeling, the poet drew near to where Master Chesei was sitting and stood gazing at him in a kind of daze. A heavy silence reigned for a long while, then suddenly the Master opened his eyes, turned to him and spoke:

"You can go now. You have not really produced what you promised at the beginning. But certainly you have produced something sufficient to entitle you to leave in safety. Do you know what it is?"

He waited.

"A warning to those who dream of revolution. If you are planning revolution, you must beware of letting songs about insubstantial revolution be sung too loudly in the streets. Day has only really broken when the whole forest is awake, the chirping of a few birds waking early does not mean that day has come."

He stood silent.

"On the contrary, the noise of those early-rising birds may make the forest's morning sleep far deeper and far longer. Often, if you go back to sleep again after waking for a moment, you fail to wake up when day comes."

Master Chesei wiped his weary eyes with a sleeve, then added in a cold voice:

"Be off with you. Before I'm tempted to blame you for this failure."

Once again, he went on his way. Walking along quiet hillside paths, with no sign of any other human being, his steps were light and quick. Shaking off the dust of the world's debates about right and wrong; like a cloud, a breeze, a wild flower, a bird.

33

Afterwards, how did his poetry change? Did his poetry, following his body, move slowly closer towards old age and death? If legends and records are both equally silent about his later life, is it because there was a reluctance to end by a mournful decline the story of a life so overflowing with humour and wit, so marked by exuberance and melancholy? Did his poetry really stagnate, as most people today believe, after a third transformation, together with his body, finally reduced to silence along some lonely and weary road?

Not at all. Fifty is known as "the age of the knowledge of heaven" and appropriately enough it was in the year he turned fifty that his poetry changed once more. That year he unexpectedly met the Old Drunkard again while he was in the Diamond Mountains and his poetry entered its last phase after long wandering.

It has not been emphasized much until now, but he had not forgotten the Old Drunkard. Though it was twenty years since they had once met and parted, when he was still young, and he had never seen him face to face in all that long period, the impression and words left by the Old Drunkard deep in his heart had not faded. Just like the Diamond Mountains, which he visited every year, as time went by the Old Drunkard came rather to seem like the birthplace of his poetic spirit, ever new, ever closer.

In fact, not many years after they had gone their separate ways, he had felt a desire to meet the Old Drunkard again. But in those first few years he mainly went wandering in the Kwanbuk and the Kwanso regions, so that even though he visited the Diamond Mountains yearly, it was no easy task to reach the Old Drunkard's inn that lay near the foot of the mountain in the Kwandong area. When he finally made up his mind and visited the place five or six years later, there was no way he could meet either the old man or the woman he lived with. When he enquired of the nearby villagers, all he could learn was that the woman was the occupier of the newly-built tomb on the sunny hillside across from the inn.

After that, whenever he visited the Diamond Mountains his heart would throb in expectation that this time he might meet the Old Drunkard, a feeling no less intense than the expectation of the magnificent scenery. When he had first met him, he was already so advanced in years that he might well have been dead by now, but for some reason he felt quite sure that the old man was still alive and waiting for him somewhere in the very heart of the mountain, united with a mysterious secret landscape that he had never so far seen. At last that year they met again.

The Old Drunkard was living in an isolated hermitage

somewhere in the Outer Diamond Mountains, true to his poetic ideals. It was a small temple run by an old acquaintance of his; there the two spent three days and three nights talking about poetry, like bosom friends who have longed for each other's company. He was surprised to see that his own ideas on poetry had moved closer to those of the Old Drunkard, which he had only vaguely understood in his youth, and he listened to him humbly. The old man received his young friend, after a long absence, with a childlike happiness and talked of the world, life, and poetry with a childlike sincerity. Their talk was no one-sided affair, though.

He had still not been able to get completely clear of the swamps of quarrelling and hatred, so that while the Old Drunkard strove to raise his poetic vision to a higher level, he in turn tried to bring the Old Drunkard's ideas about poetry back down to earth, feeling that they were soaring far too high, basing his arguments on principles derived from his own bitter experience of life's hardships. Their meeting was in many senses a union of one who had gone on ahead and one who had followed close behind; it may fairly be said that the principles agreed between them there represented the essence of a vision that the two poets had each finally attained at the end of their separate ways.

What they said to each other is difficult to capture in the words of this world; no record or report of it exists. It was the same with the poetry he composed after that. His earlier poems had presupposed an audience and had been seen as acts of dialogue, but his poetry now became a complete monologue. It is perhaps partly because there was no one listening and he himself did not preserve things, but even if he had wished to write down those last works, there was no writing system that could possibly do justice to them.

As a result his poetry, which had undergone various stages of transformation, finally had to be put into forms other than spoken words and written letters, which was no easy matter. As soon as he ceased to compose poems as acts of dialogue, he was no longer a poet as far as the world was concerned; once his poetry took on a self-oriented purpose, his fame as a poet was over, there was nobody who witnessed his last years. As far as other people were concerned, he was nothing more than an old traveller passing their village, looking half asleep and half awake, filled with a strange sense of self-contentment.

There was one exception: his second son, Ik-kyun. Three years before his death, Ik-kyun came from somewhere down in the south to bring him home; he was the last person in the world to see him and know him for what he was. Let us examine the last phase of his life and poetry by hearing how in the end Ik-kyun failed to bring his father home.

After his elder brother, Hak-kyun, had left for his foster-home, going to live with his uncle's widow, Ik-kyun grew up under his mother's care as her only remaining son. Once he had come of age and his family was more or less settled, he began to search for his father. His filial concern was less for his father in his lonely and weary wanderings than for his mother, a virtual widow abandoned to endless solitude.

Communications in those days were difficult, travel was extremely slow, so that it was no easy matter to find someone who was all the time on the move. By the time Ik-kyun reached a place where he heard that his father had been, he always found that his father had moved on. Sometimes, following a false report, he travelled hundreds of miles in vain, and once or twice he encountered imposters pretending to be his father with a hat like his and a bamboo staff, who ran off covered in shame.

What made matters even more difficult for Ik-kyun was his father's own unwillingness to return home. Twice he had found him, only to lose him again. Once, after he had found him near Andong in Kyongsang Province, his father asked Ik-kyun to get him a pair of straw shoes for the journey, then disappeared; another time they were on the way home after he had found him near Ninth Moon Mountain, in Hwanghae Province, but he slipped away while Ik-kyun was asleep.

As a result, when Ik-kyun caught up with his father for the last time at Hadong in the southern part of the country, his resolve was very firm: never to leave him alone for a moment, not once to let him out of his sight, never to be more than one step away from him, to tie their clothes together when they slept and never to sleep deeply. Underlying these resolves was a combination of pride and resentment: "It's all very well for you, enjoying yourself wandering around a whole life long, but what about me? what about Mother? You may say it was because of your grudge against the world, but don't you realize that your behaviour only breeds new grudges? Don't you realize the bitterness I felt, having to grow up hearing myself being called a fatherless bastard all the time? You don't seem to consider the anguish Mother felt, lying awake grieving all night long when the flowers bloomed in spring or the leaves fell in autumn. I wonder if you can imagine how she feels now, waiting there, her hatred and bitterness diminished with the passage of time, yearning only to see you once beside her before she dies. No. This time I'm never going to leave you alone."

Faithful to his resolve, Ik-kyun kept a really close watch on his father. When they slept, he hid his bamboo hat, his clothes, and his straw shoes; when they were awake, he never allowed himself to move more than a foot away from him. They washed their faces at the river standing side by side, and he even followed him when he went to relieve himself.

Strangely enough, the father quietly accepted his son's vigilance. He clearly revealed, though not in so many words, that this time he had no intention of thwarting his efforts. Ik-kyun was more or less encouraged in this by the fact that he was already fifty-three, too old to be a wanderer much longer, and since he was no longer composing boisterous poems there were not the crowds of people clustering around that he had seen on the previous occasions.

Two days after they began their journey home, however, Ik-kyun had a strange experience. They had just come over the mountain pass at Chupung; emerging from behind a small bush after relieving himself, Ik-kyun found that his father had disappeared from the shade of the old pine tree only five steps away where he had been sitting to get his breath back after the climb. Ik-kyun's heart turned over, and he clenched his teeth. "To the very end . . ." he thought, and began to look for a place where he might have hidden. What happened then was even more startling:

"What are you up to? Have you lost something?"

Hearing what seemed to be his father's voice, he turned, only to find him sitting exactly where he had left him.

"Did you go somewhere just now?" Ik-kyun asked, astonished at his sudden return from nowhere, but happy not to have lost him. His father looked puzzled, as he replied: "I didn't budge an inch. Why, is something wrong?"

That was precisely what Ik-kyun was wondering, and it made him feel most uneasy.

The same thing happened again soon afterwards. Over the top of a hill, they came across a small stream:

"Look!" his father called out. "Let's cool our feet in that stream over there before we go on! Haven't we gone far enough for today?"

Ik-kyun followed him to the bank of the stream, and there it happened again. Once he had watched his father take off his socks and dip his feet in the water, Ik-kyun felt reassured and let his eyes wander until a strange feeling suddenly came over him; he looked back, there was no sign of his father, who had been sitting only a few footsteps away!

Ik-kyun jumped to his feet, rushed to the top of the tallest rock he could see, and was gazing around, when he heard his father's voice coming from where he had last seen him:

"Now what are you up to? Is something wrong?"

Ik-kyun looked down, and there was his father gazing up at him and rubbing his feet in the water with both hands.

It was only after he had experienced the same kind of incident a few more times that Ik-kyun began vaguely to sense a possible reason for such strange phenomena. The next day, while they were walking along at the foot of a rocky hill, Ik-kyun deliberately moved away, watching to see how his father could disappear like that. His father simply sat down to rest on a slab of rock jutting out from the slope, but Ik-kyun was only a few steps away before his shape began to grow hazy. Startled, he continued on a few more paces.

His father was gone again! But on closer examination, he saw that he was wrong; his father was undoubtedly still sitting where he had been, but having removed his hat and gazing skywards at the clouds, he looked exactly like a rock! A rock, moreover, that had been there for thousands of years and was all overgrown with green moss! It seemed that he had been unable to see him there because he blended so perfectly with the natural surroundings.

Then there was another peculiar and mysterious thing that occurred as they journeyed on together. It involved his father's poetry. In times past, Ik-kyun had simply pretended not to notice when his father began to mutter things to himself. He had guessed it might be poetry, but his father was not addressing anyone in particular, and since he had not had a proper education Ik-kyun could not make sense even of those parts he heard. Indeed, the thought that it might have been this very poetry that had drawn his father away from home provoked in him a silent revulsion.

One day, though, when his father began to mutter something he felt differently. Maybe because of the surprising events of the last few days, he felt that there must be some kind of out-of-the-ordinary meaning to the muttering. For the first time in his life, Ik-kyun asked his father about his poetry:

"I said that flower over there is beautiful."

His father pointed at a rock face by the side of the road with a vague expression. When his father raised his finger, there was undoubtedly simply a red cliff there – but suddenly it seemed that a crimson cuckoopint broke through the stone in full bloom. That was not the only time. Eager to discover more about the mysterious power of his father's muttering, Ik-kyun began to ask questions whenever he heard it, and had similar experiences every time.

"That cloud up there is floating peacefully." His father explained, and following his pointing finger he saw a splendid cloud appear in the hitherto empty sky, finer than any he had ever seen, and float there quietly.

"I said those carp are swimming in leisurely style."

His father had no sooner said that, than he saw in the water a few carp swimming in leisurely style near the bank in a spot where a moment before there had been nothing visible, as if conjured up by his father's pointing finger. When his father recited something about birds, the most lovely bird would fly out from somewhere and chirp gaily; when he recited something about the wind, the coolest of winds would come blowing, drying the sweat on their brows.

After a while, Ik-kyun began to formulate a vague explanation for these things. His father's poetry did not really make things appear from nowhere, it simply made apparent what had been there all the time. But that was the full extent of his understanding, and to the very end Ik-kyun was unable to figure out why he always had the impression of things materializing from nowhere.

Once he had become more observant, Ik-kyun noticed many other inexplicable things. This was especially the case when his father mingled with other people, in a market for example. As soon as his father was among people, he stood out as the shabbiest, weariest old man of all. Like a dead plant in the very middle of a field full of spring flowers. It was the same when he spoke. The mysterious power he had when muttering poetry seemed to vanish, so that people could not understand what he was saying and needed Ik-kyun to interpret for them. It was unbelievable that such a father had not starved to death before now in the course of his wanderings.

It was the sixth day of their journey. Having passed through Kyongsang Province, they had stopped for the night in a village at the foot of Chuknyong Pass. Up to that point, Ik-kyun had been full of the idea of bringing his father home; but suddenly a question struck him: "What is Father, really? Am I doing the right thing in bringing this kind of a father back home?" This question had slowly formed in Ik-kyun's mind as a result of the last few days' events.

People had told him that his father was a poet. But for Ik-kyun as a child, a poem meant the same as a curse. Sometimes they had called his father "a wanderer", but such people had bodies out of all proportion with their heads.

To Ik-kyun, who had trained himself since earliest childhood to give more weight to the real side of things, that name meant nothing more than "a beggar". To rescue his father from those two misfortunes had been Ik-kyun's sole intention in setting out to accomplish his simple filial duty. It was far removed from his deep care for his lonely mother, but marked by the same kind of sincerity.

At the time of his first encounter with his father, Ik-kyun had already begun to feel some doubt as to whether his father's situation was really a misfortune or a curse. His reluctance to return to his family seemed to spring from a fear of losing what he had so far enjoyed; Ik-kyun considered that pleasure less as something positive than as a passive shunning of responsibility on his father's part, all those responsibilities, ranging from productivity, earning a living, and bringing up a family to the educated man's functions in society at large, that his father had rejected from early on. Therefore he reckoned that if his father was afraid of something, it must be of questions about the responsibilities he had shunned in the past, responsibilities that he would necessarily have to assume on returning home now.

Despite the two subterfuges his father had used to escape from him, Ik-kyun's intentions had not changed much. If there was any change at all, it was from a sense that his father was not only afraid but bewitched. He reckoned that his father was being led by that kind of inscrutable force that necessarily accompanies misfortunes and curses, great or small.

Around the fifth day, however, Ik-kyun's heart began to feel burdened and oppressed at the sight of his father, as he slowly realized that he was not bewitched at all, but was actually enjoying himself. Would he be able to make clouds move and flowers bloom, once back in his own shabby room with its thatched roof? Would he still be able to live lofty and indifferent like some old pine tree or a moss-covered rock, once supported by the labours of Ik-kyun, his wife, and mother, and doing his own share of trivial housekeeping chores? Would his father still be able to be a poet, in the midst of cold stares directed at an old failure come home to prepare for death, or surrounded by a throng of third-rate poets drawn like moths around a light to the faded name of someone who in youth had been famous? Would he still be able to be a poet?

Deep in such thoughts, Ik-kyun lay next to his father, who had been snoring since early in the evening, but he could not get to sleep. Their shared blood inevitably induced an understanding of a higher kind than any that his little learning could bestow, and Ik-kyun found himself driven into an abrupt crisis of hesitation.

All the while, his father kept snoring. As the night wore on and the murmured whispers of the innkeeper and his wife in their room finally ceased, all fell silent. Amidst the stillness, Ik-kyun too laid aside his thoughts and, without realizing it, fell asleep.

How much time passed? Ik-kyun had scarcely dozed off when he opened his eyes to a strange sense of emptiness. There was nobody lying beside him, while he could hear somebody making a rustling noise in the far corner of the room. It must be Father, he intuitively felt. He must be picking up his hat and coat, that Ik-kyun had not bothered to hide that night.

For some reason, Ik-kyun did not want to sit up. Rather, "At last . . ." an unidentifiable feeling of resignation first rose in him, then all the energy drained from his body. Besides, the returning thoughts of the previous hours neutralized the resolve with which he had left home, and which had been confirmed when he first found him.

Meanwhile Father's packing seemed to be complete; he moved towards the door. "Now I must get up . . ." Ik-kyun felt a secret anxiety but still he could not make his body rise from its place. Suddenly his father's movements stopped.

Though it was pitch dark, Ik-kyun felt a kind of sunny warmth on his face for a while. "Father's looking down at me!" he thought, and he shut his eyes furtively, as if to escape his father's unseen gaze.

When Ik-kyun opened his eyes again, it was because he heard the door opening. In the pale light of the waning moon outside, he could see his father's bent silhouette as he left the room, wearing his bamboo hat. Before he stepped down on to the garden path, his father turned and glanced back, as if he knew that his son was awake.

When Ik-kyun finally stood up, gathering all his strength to break the mysterious spell that had paralysed him, the sound of his father's footsteps in the garden was dying away. Seized with a sudden sense of urgency, Ik-kyun scrambled to the doorway and, hanging on to it, he called out:

"Father!"

But it was as if his voice had been silenced by the sight of his father's back, and no sound issued from his lips. The man moving away in the glimmering darkness was not his father. He was a poet, and nothing else. A poet tied down by nothing in the whole world. His father moved beyond the brushwood gate of the inn and stepped on to the grassy forest trail; at that very moment he vanished completely. "Has he turned into a tree? Or a rock? Or a white briar rose? Or the early morning mist now beginning to thicken . . .?" As those thoughts came to him, Ik-kyun quickly changed his still unspoken words of protest into a blessing:

"Farewell. May you ever find peace and plenty in your poetry."

That was father and son's last parting in this world.

34

Now, what remains to be told? His death a few years later? Ik-kyun's admirable sense of filial duty in moving his father's bones from somewhere down in Cholla Province to a tomb at Yongwol in Kangwon Province? The quarrels among people of later generations about what they selectively remember in the things he showed? All useless. What we set out to trace was one man's life as a poet; now that quest is over.

What we have seen through Ik-kyun's eyes is a man fulfilled as a poet; as was mentioned earlier, any further search by means of words, spoken or written, is pointless.

His death, too, which followed soon after? Well, to end on a blunt note: a dead poet is no poet.

Brief ENCOUNTERS

Short books. *Timeless stories.*

Louisa May Alcott
Behind a Mask

Margery Allingham
The Case of the Late Pig

Margaret Atwood
Significant Moments

Jane Austen
Lady Susan

J. G. Ballard
Venus Smiles

Simone de Beauvoir
Woman of Genius

Ingmar Bergman
Sunday's Children

Roberto Bolaño
Distant Star

Jorge Luis Borges
The Book of Imaginary Beings

Richard Brautigan
In Watermelon Sugar

Mikhail Bulgakov
The Fatal Eggs

Toni Cade Bambara
First Light

Italo Calvino
The Castle of Crossed Destinies

Angela Carter
A Souvenir of Japan

Vera Caspary
Laura

Eileen Chang
Young at the Time

Colette
The Cat

Arthur Conan Doyle
The Parasite

Anita Desai
Fire on the Mountain

Charles Dickens and Wilkie Collins
The Lazy Tour of Two Idle Apprentices

Fyodor Dostoevsky
A Gentle Spirit and A Faint Heart

Fumiko Enchi
Masks

F. Scott Fitzgerald
The Curious Case of Benjamin Button

Graham Greene
The Third Man

Jacqueline Harpman
We Were Forbidden

Ernest Hemingway
The Old Man and the Sea

Brief ENCOUNTERS

Short books. *Timeless stories.*

Bohumil Hrabal
Dancing Lessons for the Advanced in Age

Aldous Huxley
Ape and Essence

Christopher Isherwood
Sally Bowles

James Joyce
The Dead

Franz Kafka
Mouse Folk

Yasunari Kawabata
The Master of Go

Nella Larsen
Passing

Halldór Laxness
A Parish Chronicle

Ursula K. Le Guin
Paradises Lost

H. P. Lovecraft
The Dunwich Horror

Herman Melville
Bartleby, the Scrivener

Toni Morrison
Recitatif

Haruki Murakami
Pinball, 1973

Ngũgĩ wa Thiong'o
Fighters and Martyrs

Georges Perec
Things

José Saramago
Cain

Mary Shelley
The Invisible Girl

Natsume Sōseki
An Undesirable Friend

Gertrude Stein
Tender Buttons

Bram Stoker
Dracula's Guest

Dylan Thomas
Portrait of the Artist as a Young Dog

Kurt Vonnegut
Monkey Business

Edith Wharton
Bewitched

Virginia Wool
Kew Gard

Richar
Down